Zinnia

A MONSTER MILLIONAIRE ROMANCE

SOFIA ROSE

Other Books by Sofia

<u>SOFIA ROSE</u>

<u>Fortune Records Omegaverse:</u>

Snapdragon

Aster

Iris

Zinnia

Fritillaria

<u>Briar Hill Omegaverse:</u>

Touched & Tamed

<u>Whimsywood Tales:</u>

A Teacup for Trouble

<u>The Zodiac Society:</u>

Patreon exclusive, 13 novellas

A Note on Omegaverse

Before you begin, I wanted to take a moment to explain the version of omegaverse you'll find in this series.

Omegaverse is a romance subgenre that originated in fanfiction spaces and has since evolved into many different interpretations across books and authors. There is no single "correct" version. What follows is *my* take on omegaverse, and the rules that apply specifically to the world of the *Fortune Records Omegaverse*.

In this universe, society is divided between humans and monsters, who have historically lived apart. Because of this separation, humans do not grow up knowing about omegaverse dynamics. Human characters are unaware of secondary genders, heats, mating bonds, and related biology until they spend meaningful time with monsters. For humans, a dormant secondary gender is only triggered through meeting a monster mate.

Secondary Genders

In addition to primary sex, characters in this world have a secondary gender: **alpha** or **omega**. Any primary gender can be alphas or omegas. There are **no betas** in this universe.

Among monsters, secondary gender can be sensed instinctively. Humans do not have this ability in the same way, though some humans may experience a faint or inconsistent awareness of a mate. Monsters, particularly shifters, have heightened senses of smell, which makes their ability to scent secondary gender and mates far stronger and more reliable.

Omegas are not publicly labeled or categorized within human society.

Scent

Both alphas and omegas have distinct, unique scents, often influenced by personality, emotional state, and individual biology. A mate's scent is instinctively recognizable and often irresistible, creating a powerful pull between bonded partners.

When an omega becomes aroused, their scent sweetens, intensifying attraction and instinctual responses in nearby alphas. Scent plays a central role in attraction, bonding, and recognition throughout this world.

Heats and Instinct

Omegas experience heats, which are biological periods marked by heightened desire, sensitivity, and instinct. These urges often begin as an intensification of emotion and attraction, and can escalate into overwhelming instinct while in heat. Choice and consent still exist, but biology plays a powerful role in shaping how these experiences feel and unfold.

Mates and Bonds

Omegaverse bonds in this world are biological and deeply rooted in instinct. An omega will only ever be bonded to one alpha, and may also bond with additional omega mates within the same bond structure.

To complete a bond, two things must occur: a verbal acceptance of the bond, and a **claiming bite** from the alpha. The bite itself is pleasurable for the omega and marks the bond as fully formed. Until both acceptance and the bite occur, the bond remains incomplete.

Anatomy and Knotting

Male alphas in this universe have knots as part of their anatomy. A knot is an expanding ring of tissue around the base of an alpha's penis that swells during orgasm. This is a biological trait associated with mating and bonding.

Pack Structure

Pack dynamics in this world consist of one alpha with one or more omegas. These dynamics are instinctual rather than societal, and individual relationships may look very different depending on the characters involved.

This note is not meant to be exhaustive, but rather to offer grounding before you begin. As with all omegaverse stories, much of how these elements function is revealed through character experience, emotion, and connection.

Thank you for reading, and I hope you enjoy this world as much as I loved writing it.

Content Warning

The following book contains content that may be triggering for some readers. There are themes of segregation. There is also mention of a severe allergy and extreme allergic reaction.

Content includes: primal play, omegaverse, knotting, anal penetration, pegging, Dom/sub dynamic, switch dynamic.

If you need any more information on any of the above, you can email me at sofiaroseauthor@gmail.com

Dedication

For my Orc lovers, you know who you are.

Chapter 1

Rosie

Shutting the door and clicking the lock into place, I take a deep breath as I flip the sign to signal that we are closed for the day.

Today was busy, Farrow and Ben swept off their feet enough that I had to step in and help. I've been trying to take a step back from the hands on tasks of running my café, but it's been tough to let go. I probably need to hire a new member for the team. Maybe that's something I can look at tonight.

I take a moment to look around my little space. The florist's selection sits empty, the last bouquet sold a couple hours ago. It's set in the grocer's section, as I have aptly named it. It's a marketplace for local producers, a range of crafted items and pantry foods.

I've tried to keep things local, even the pretty menu board with hand drawn roses is a piece by a local artist. My brass-toned register shines, the late afternoon light reflected in its freshly cleaned surface. It sits on my marble top counters, the fridges mostly empty for the end of the day.

The plush velvet seating is an annoyance to clean, but it is beautiful and so cozy to sit in. I want to curl up there with a coffee right now, but I have things to do. The stairs to my apartment are tucked away, you have to walk through the store room to get to them. It's a blessing in disguise because otherwise I would never notice when we are running out of things. Life running a café can get pretty busy.

My café is a mix of pink, burgundy, gold and marble, with green plants dotted throughout the space. It's a refined pallet.

My apartment on the other hand, is a clash of every color in the rainbow. I'm greeted by my bright yellow walls and knick knacks scattered about the place. My home is where I can comfortably make a mess and just relax.

I slip off my apron and hang it on the back of my door. Time to get changed out of these grubby clothes. Hopping in the shower, I make quick work of getting into a fresh outfit. I throw on some jeans and sneakers with a light sweater.

The drive to Flora's house is a solid thirty minutes, but the view is nice. The weather is turning to fall, the leaves on the trees beginning to turn a yellow ocher. There's still some warmth in the air, and my AC is on while I drive.

The fall leaves remind me of change, and things have certainly changed in the city this past year. This is my second fall since monsters and humans have started to mingle with one another.

We were a city divided, and we still mostly are. I have only seen a monster in the human side of town once, and I can almost guarantee that there are no humans wandering about their side either. I'm heading to the small suburb that has grown in between over the last year, home to both humans and monsters.

My best friend happened to be one of the first humans to meet a monster. Flora and her mate, Sebastian, met at a photo shoot. I can't help the giggle that escapes me when I remember how much she thought he hated her initially. Turns out, he was head over heels.

Thinking about them makes the pang of loneliness in my chest return. I have everything I wanted, I've worked hard for my café to be what it is and that was all I dreamed of.

I should be feeling fulfilled, right?

Flora's new house looms above me as I press the button on my buzzer to open the gate. It's a stunning new build, and I have been overseeing the decorating process while she and Sebastian have been on tour.

My best friend and her mate just also happen to be incredibly famous musicians.

Flora had gone through everything meticulously with the interior designer, and I have been keeping an eye on things. Today was just a final walk through before they come home tomorrow.

Besides, I also wanted to leave them a little gift for when they arrive.

The house is purely Flora's aesthetic, Sebastian happy for her to do her thing when it came to the decorating. Every wall is a light pastel shade, the furniture brighter pops of color. Setting the bottle of champagne down on the counter, I take out my clipboard, pop on my headphones, and get to work on double checking the project list.

Chapter 2

Finnegan

I pull up to the address that my assistant, Cynthia, gave me. There's a small bright red car in the driveway that must be Flora's. Sebastian isn't quite as big as me, but he for sure wouldn't fit into that vehicle.

The gate is open so I pull in and park. If Sebastian isn't home this will ruin how I wanted this to go. I'm dropping off a gift for them both now that they're back from tour.

Tickets sold well, nearly every show was sold out. Which was more than we expected for the first tour with both human and monster performers. But the sentiment overall has been that if the show was in a human area, the audience would mostly leave after Flora's set. The same for the monster areas, Sebastian had told me that people would show up much later just to hear his set.

I really appreciated them pushing forward with their performances, and still acting like it was a packed out venue each night. The whole label appreciated it, really. As the Director of Label Strategy for Fortune Records, the least I could do was personally come by with some flowers.

They wouldn't be in this mess if it weren't for me. It was my big idea to push them to do the tour. Heck, it was my idea to merge the human and monster sides of the label in the first place. I'm not going to beat myself up about that one though. Despite the hiccups along the way, seeing all of these mates find one another has been the very tip of the iceberg on the benefits from the merger.

I shake my head, clearing my thoughts as I get out of the car and grab the flowers Cynthia picked out.

The door to the house is unlocked, pushing open when I try to knock. Shit, I hope everything is OK. I call out a quick hello, but no one answers. With no car in the driveway for Sebastian, I wonder if they've gone out and left the house unlocked. That would be a very unusual thing for a dragon shifter like Sebastian to do. He would certainly be more protective of his home than that.

Walking inside, I shut the door behind myself and wander through the main foyer. Surely if someone was home they would have sniffed me out by now.

Speaking of scents, the most delicious notes of a deep red wine hit my nose, my mouth beginning to water. I've never smelled something so decadent. I follow it, my nose twitching and tightening the skin against my tusks.

The scent leads me to the kitchen. A woman is standing there, her back to me with a pair of headphones on. No wonder she didn't hear me. Her pretty face fills with fear as she turns, not expecting to see me standing behind her.

I should be reassuring her, doing something to explain why I am there. But all I can do is stare.

Her chocolate brown hair sparkles, the warm lighting picking out red and golden tones. Her eyes are the bright cerulean blue of the ocean on a perfect day. Her hips are full and soft, the tight jeans she wears hugging her in all the right places.

The scent is clearer now, all of the spice and fruity complexity of a warm and rich red wine. Not just any scent, her omega scent.

This is my mate.

My brain fully catches up with the moment, and I realize that I am currently scaring the shit out of her.

"Hi, sorry, I didn't mean to scare you." I hold out a placating hand, almost gesturing at the completely friendly flowers in my other. "I'm just bringing a gift. I work with Sebastian and Flora. I thought that they would be home."

Her chest slows down slightly, her breathing calming as she takes me in again.

"You gave me a fright!" She places a hand on her chest, a little dramatic but charming. "Sorry, but they're not back yet."

"The tour finished a week ago." I'm surprised that they're still away, I thought that they must just be out for the day.

"Yeah, they were getting the house renovated while they were away." She gestures around us to the freshly cleaned space. "But the final touches were delayed, so they went to the beach for a week."

I don't say anything, completely mesmerized by this beautiful creature. She was pretty average height for a human, if I were to compare her to the others I have met. But she still feels tiny, even with the distance between us.

"You can leave those here if you'd like." My mate points to the flowers still clutched in my hand. "They're back tomorrow so they'll stay nice for them."

I nod, letting her take them from my hand. Her smell is overwhelming as she gets close. I knew that your omega's scent was supposed to be attractive, but this is like a drug. How am I supposed to leave now that I've found her?

"Is that what you do?" I ask quickly before she can tell me to leave.

"What? I don't understand." Her thick brows furrow again and I realize that she had moved on in the conversation.

"The renovation. Are you their designer?" I need to know everything about this small human in front of me. Firstly, being how she is connected to Sebastian and Flora.

"Oh, no!" She laughs and it is a beautiful twinkle in the air. I need to hear it again. "I'm Rosie, Flora's friend! I was keeping an eye on the project while they were away."

Rosie. A beautiful name for a beautiful woman.

"Right. Well then, I might see you around again." She says when I don't reply. "If you work with Flora. Anyway, I need to head back to work. You go on ahead and I'll lock up."

I can't think of anything to say to her, her dismissal clear. She's right though, I know her name and her connection to Flora, surely I can seek her out again. This time a little more prepared.

The walk to my car feels wrong. It's one of the hardest things I've done to start the engine and drive away from my mate so soon after finding her.

Chapter 3

Rosie

I watch through the window as he gets into his sleek, expensive looking SUV. Only once he has pulled out on to the street and I hear the noise of his engine fade do I sink to the floor.

Fuck. He scared the life out of me.

I've only ever met one monster as tall as that, the kraken in Sebastian's band. But I think this male was an orc. I've met Flora's friend Tabitha before, and she looked quite similar. She said she was an orc when I asked.

He had deep green skin and black hair, with *tusks* coming out of his mouth. Surprisingly, he was very attractive. I've been interested in a few of the monsters I've met so far, but he is probably the hottest one. He was wearing a tight fitting black suit, like he just came from a very fancy office. Surely he doesn't wear that to the studio?

He had said that he worked with Flora and Sebastian, but that suit makes me wonder in what capacity. He's not like, super important, is he?

He *felt* super important. And I had this strange feeling as he left, like I wanted him to stay, but that was irrational.

Moving through the steps almost robotically, I grab my things from the counter. The vase of zinnias stare up at me in their bright orange and pink hues. I need to get out of here. I quickly lock up the house, and get on the road.

My thoughts keep straying to the male. I must have left the front door unlocked and that was how he got in. Shit, how could I have been so stupid as to waltz around an expensive house, door unlocked, and music on full blast.

I'm lucky that he was friendly. Or at least, that he didn't hurt me. What if he had been trouble?

Chapter 4

Finnegan

I can't stop thinking about her.

My mate.

I wish she was here right now, that I could be doused in her decadent scent.

A cold shower helped to clear my head a little. I need to focus if I am going to figure out what to do here.

Rosie... I know I have heard something about a Rosie. Surely she has come up in conversation at the studio?

Moving through the steps of my evening routine, I set out my mug for my morning coffee on the counter. I can be a bit grumpy before my first sip of it, so it's best that I prep ahead.

Coffee... something niggles at the back of my brain, the color pink appearing before the actual cup itself.

Rosie's café!

The cups, I've seen the takeout coffee cups with her logo on them around the studio. It's coming back to me now. Flora's friend who owns the café on the human side of town. People rave about her blends and humans bring her coffee in to the studio for their monster coworkers.

Wow, my mate is perfect. She runs her own business? And to think, it's a café, when I love coffee so much. We're matched so well.

I think.

OK, so I don't know anything else about her. Yet. I can figure this out.

I grab my laptop as I get into bed and open the browser, searching for 'Rosie's café'.

The map location and company website is the first result, followed by a few articles on the opening of the café. I spend some time reading, learning about how she supports local makers. She's incredible.

Scrolling back up, I consider the map location again. I could just go, couldn't I? There are no rules preventing me from going to the human side of town. I could just go to her café. Tomorrow, even.

Yes, that sounds like a fantastic idea. I can figure out some excuse or reason before then.

Chapter 5

Rosie

The morning rush hasn't exactly been much of a rush. A slow group of caffeine deprived customers have tiptoed around, but the tables have only been half full. I like these kinds of mornings, despite the fact that they're not great for business.

It means that I get to sit and enjoy my own café as if I am the customer.

Once I'm sure that I can leave Farrow and Ben to handle things on their own, I brew myself a quick cappuccino and sit in a booth at the back.

I love this spot. I can sit and watch the world go by. It's not often that I actually get to relax in the café and enjoy my coffee.

The plush velvet booth seat barely resists my shoulders as I sink back against it. I am struck again by how much I love this space. It's been my baby for almost two years now. I can still remember how excited I was when I got the keys.

It was a fluke really, that I could afford it. I don't come from money, and I never would have been able to satisfy a dream like this on my own. It wasn't an ideal set of circumstances that brought me to buying my café though.

The whole time back then was a blur. Flora and I had just finished college, and we were still living in our tiny one bedroom apartment near campus. My nut allergy has always made me anxious, but that day Flora and I went out to eat without my EpiPen. That part was my fault, and I totally get that. But in my defense, we were going to eat in a restaurant that was supposedly 100% allergen free, hence why I wasn't quite so anxious as usual.

I even double checked with them that I had a peanut allergy. But that didn't stop me from going into anaphylactic shock. Luckily, Flora knew what was up and immediately called the emergency services. I was given adrenaline, but it was too late.

My body shut down completely, and my heart stopped. The paramedics had to use a defibrillator and literally zap me back to life. It's weird, but I feel at peace with the whole experience at this point. The payout from the lawsuit meant that I got some fancy ass therapy, so I'm sure that also helped.

But more than anything, I was able to get my beautiful café and I wouldn't trade that for the world. I still built this place from the ground up to what it is today. The building that I bought was a concrete hell hole. But I worked with a designer who brought my vision to life.

Things were going well for me here. I didn't have the cost of the space, because I bought it myself without a mortgage. It's been like this for a while though, and that makes me wonder if I should be doing something to make the space grow.

The last time I felt like this was when I put in the grocer's section a year ago. The itch to do something else has begun and I'm not sure what it should be. I could afford to hire on a manager now, or even promote Farrow who has been with me since day one. But then what would I do with my days.

So yes, I liked slow mornings where I could sit and absorb my happy place. Even if it was bad for business. These days interspersed between the hectic ones truly help me to feel grateful for these moments when I get them.

Taking a step back and hiring on a manager would make days like this feel boring. No matter the itch, I don't feel ready for that yet.

I'm pulled from my thoughts by a panicked Farrow, her bright pink hair standing out even in my café.

"I need your help!" Her voice is shaky and I look around the peaceful café to see what could be bothering her, or who.

Except the café isn't as peaceful as it just was. A wide berth has formed around one particular table.

I blink quickly, thinking that I must be hallucinating. Because there is no sane reason that the orc from yesterday would be sitting in my café reading a paper like he was here every day.

He completely ignores the group of onlookers, focusing on his paper, his brow furrowed in concentration. His hair is swept back today, revealing a pointy pair of green ears.

Farrow grips my arm tightly, a tremor working its way through me from her.

"OK," I pat her on the shoulder and gesture to my half drank coffee. "Sit down until you feel a bit better, and then clean this up."

Moving her into my seat, I grab a menu from the counter and make my way to the tall male.

"Good morning," I put on a chirpy voice. I'm not scared of him like Farrow is. I've met plenty of monsters by now, and if this one was going to hurt me he already had ample opportunity.

"Ah, morning." He folds his paper, setting it down on the shiny brass-topped table.

I give him the menu, listing out the specials for the day, "I'll be back to take your order in a minute."

"That's not necessary." He barely glances at the pink and gold foiled card. "I'll take whatever you think is most delicious."

The laugh escapes me before I can stop it.

"I'm serious." His grin nearly has me on the floor. As if his pointed tusks weren't enough, bright white teeth with fanged canines sparkle at me. A warmth forms in my stomach that I can't really explain.

"Well, in that case," I can't help my answering grin. "Any allergies?"

"None."

"Alright. One surprise breakfast coming right up!"

I head back to the kitchen, writing his ticket as I go. I know just what to order for him.

Not to overtly brag, but my avocado toast is award winning. No, literally. I won an award for 'Best Dish' in a city wide competition just last month. The thrill of saying that hasn't worn off.

Farrow is still resting in the back, watching the orc and biting her lip in what I can only assume is anxiety. She'll realize soon that he's harmless.

Chapter 6

F*innegan*

My mate shines, a glowing ball of energy as she whizzes about the space.

I had forgotten to come up with an excuse to be here, instead just showing up and hoping for the best. Rosie easily accepted me into the café.

I didn't realize until she walked away after taking my 'order' how nervous I was that she would turn me away. I'm not sure that I really could have handled that.

Luckily, she took my jest for what it was, and presented me with a colorful plate of avocado toast and a latte.

Being served by my mate in this capacity was much stranger than I had thought to anticipate. I know that I shouldn't be infiltrating her workplace like this. Hell, I can see that none of the humans are particularly happy that I'm here. So I am completely aware that I am bad for business right now.

But I just couldn't help myself. I needed to see her again.

Last night was torture. I lay awake thinking about her kind, bright blue eyes. Her soft and shining hair. The little freckles dotted about the bridge of her nose.

The need to protect, to take her away, to bite and fuck her until she loses all sense and accepts me as her mate…

Shaking my head, I take a bite of my food. A delicious burst of lime and hot honey flits over my tongue. She really wasn't kidding when she took my request for the most delicious thing on the menu.

The richness of her scent cuts through as she veers near, taking an order from a brave couple who chose not to sit too far from me. I owe them big time.

Decadent spiced wine permeates my soul as I inhale. The thumping sound in my ears slows down as I relax in the presence of my mate.

Everything in this glorious café is attuned to her scent. It makes me wonder how much she works in here. I can imagine her here, every day, serving customers with her warm smile.

She wears a soft-toned pink apron, the ties cinching her waist and showing off her delicious curves. When she turns I can see her ass clearly in the same tight fitting style of jeans that she wore yesterday.

She is bubbly and friendly in her work, greeting nearly every customer as they enter. It's easy to tell that she is the spirit of this place. Rosie is beautiful like this, in her element.

I wonder what her personality is like when she isn't performing for customers. Is she just as warm and friendly? Is she grumpy like me before her morning coffee?

I want to learn her, find out what pleases her, protect and care for her.

The young human man working comes to take my plate. I had wanted to stay for longer, but that delicious plate of food was too easy to polish off quickly.

"Would you like your check?" The Human asks. I can tell by the shake in his voice that I'm making him nervous.

Giving him a close-lipped smile, I ask him to bring me a tasty dessert. I'm quickly presented with a slice of pistachio flavored cheesecake. I order another latte while he's dropping it off.

I guess I'm having a big breakfast today.

Chapter 7

Rosie

I try my best to focus on the other customers in my café, but I can't escape the glaring green in my peripheral.

Of course he had to be green.

The one color that would really stand out in my space.

If I'm being honest myself, it's not the glaring color that catches my eye. It's that every time I truly look, I can see that he's staring at me. He politely glances away, but that doesn't stop me from missing him doing it.

A strange pull in my gut tethers me to him. I normally wait on the tables in the back when Ben is working. But today I can't help but race to the tables in the front before Ben does. That is, every table but *his*.

I didn't deliver his food to him, but I could see how quickly he ate it, a pleased look on his face. It was weirdly satisfying.

I mean, people eating my recipes is normally very satisfying. But this was something else entirely. Heat bloomed through me, and I was kind of turned on..?

I took a minute off the floor, now sitting in the back room, reconsidering all of my life choices. Why was I so hot? The air had been crisp today, the first properly cold day of the season. Until that orc decided to come into my café.

Now that I think about it, it is kind of strange that he knew where to find me after yesterday. I suppose I did tell him my name.

He was talking about what I did for a living, but I don't remember telling him this.

I know on a logical level that this is really weird, but it doesn't feel that way in my gut. And I don't know how to process that.

One thing I can get annoyed at him for is how his presence is affecting my business. People have been walking into my café, seeing him there, and walking right back out again. OK, it's more so running out again.

Surprisingly there are some people staying.

I can't hide in here forever, so I head back out to help Farrow and Ben.

He's gone. His table cleared already.

Ben rushes up to me excitedly.

"Ro! He left a five hundred dollar tip. Said it was to cover any losses from people leaving."

"He what?" I can't believe what I'm hearing. Who spends five hundred dollars on *breakfast*?

"You didn't accept it though, right?"

Ben curls in on himself a little as he stares at me. "Um..."

Shit. I'm going to have to find a way to return it to him.

Chapter 8

Finnegan

Glancing at the time on the bottom of the screen, I know that I'm not going to make it to Rosie's café today.

There's an ache in my chest with that realization.

I would be more annoyed about it if this meeting was unnecessary, but it isn't. The merger between the human and monster sides of the label was my idea. So I need to be present for all the reports.

Despite the mixed feelings after Sebastian and Flora's joint tour, our profits are at a record high. Every day I count my lucky stars that they released that song together in the first few weeks of the merger. That shit was genius.

Speaking of Sebastian, my phone pings with a text from him to say thank you for the gift. I try my best to hide my chuckle, knowing that they got home and would have seen the gift yesterday. I'm sure he was keeping his mate *very* busy in their new home.

Thinking of them puts a pang in my chest again. I need to think of a better way to see Rosie. Something other than creeping on her in her workplace.

A party could do the trick…

As soon as my meeting finishes, I email Liliana to ask her to come up to my office.

The lithe Succubus, and my Head of PR, glides into the room. Her red and black coloring complimenting the dark wood tones of my office.

"Liliana. Please, take a seat."

It's our usual routine, in which she pretends to respect me and I pretend that I believe her. It's not that I think she has anything against me personally, I just don't think that Liliana has time for males in general. Unfortunately, I understand that completely.

"I need you to plan a party for me." I direct, as she takes out her notebook. "To celebrate the successful tour that Sebastian and Flora just had."

She raises her eyebrow at that, a hint of a smirk on her lips.

"When were you thinking of hosting?"

"Tomorrow."

Liliana puts her pen down, looking straight at me with her chin tilted in defiance. "Tomorrow?"

"Yes."

She sighs, but continues her note taking, albeit more aggressively.

I know that she will complain about it, but the crux of the matter is that she won't be the one actually doing the work anyway. We talk through the details, deciding it will be hosted here at the studio.

Once Liliana is gone, I give Sebastian a call to tell him about it. I make sure to insist that he and Flora invite their friends, especially any of the humans.

I feel a little guilty that I am arranging all this just to see Rosie again. But there is some good coming from it too, we probably should have planned something to celebrate the first monster and human tour anyway.

I can barely contain my excitement to see my mate tomorrow.

Chapter 9

R *osie*

Flora and I sit knee to knee on her plush new sofa. It's divine.

Although I am terrified of spilling my tea on the supple green leather.

"Did I tell you about Nereus' secret lake house?" Flora gushes, leaning forward and whispering quietly. There's no one around, we're in her home and Sebastian is off in another room, but I love the need to act conspicuous when having a good gossip.

"Yes! And that he's building the ballet studio? It's so adorable, who knew he was such a softie?"

"I had my suspicions," she giggles, leaning back against the seat with a sigh, her golden hair floating around her shoulders. "Well that's all the juicy things I can think of right now."

"You say that like we haven't been talking for two hours!" I had come over with a full stock of my special tea blends, and we had made our way through three pots while chatting. I'm not really sure why, but I choose not to bring up the whole situation with the orc.

I've missed my friend, and bringing that up will take away from spending this time together right now. It's so good to have her back home. It's great that she's successful, and I'm proud of her, but I do wish that she wouldn't have to go away for months at a time.

"Thank you again for managing all this, Ro." Flora gestures around at the fully decorated living space. "You're literally the absolute best."

"Are you kidding? Of course I managed the project! No one knows your taste better than me!" A grin spreads across my face thinking of anyone else trying to understand Flora in the aesthetics department, her mate included.

Speaking of her mate, Sebastian tiptoes into the room, his phone in his hand.

"Sorry to interrupt..." Sebastian had been under strict orders from Flora to give us a few hours of pure girl time. Not that either of us really minded him here. "But I think you'll want as much notice as possible."

Flora and I both perk up in our seats like a pair of meerkats.

"I got a call from the label," Sebastian continues. "They're hosting a party to celebrate the tour. It'll be at the studio tomorrow night, Finnegan said to bring our friends."

Sebastian looks pointedly at me when he says that last part.

Flora squeals, as she usually does when presented with any information that's remotely exciting. "Yes! You *have* to come, Rosie!"

"As if I'd miss out on a party with a bunch of hot musicians." What does she take me for, seriously?

"That's my girl!" Flora pats my head.

Sebastian busts out in laughter at the ridiculousness of it. He plonks himself down on an arm chair across from us, pouring himself a cup of tea from the pot.

Did I mention that the furniture in this house was massive? Hence why I'm practically being swallowed by this couch.

Sebastian doesn't have his wings out right now, but as a dragon shifter, he is still a huge person. He towers over Flora and I, in a mass of dark skin and glittering scales. I remember when I first saw the picture of him at that night club with Flora. When the photos from their Noma shoot came in.

I've always found him very attractive, but that's totally softened now that he's mated to my best friend. We have a nice, almost sibling-like camaraderie now.

"You don't want a musician." Sebastian says as he takes a comical sip from the tiny cup.

Flora and I share a glance. Is Sebastian trying to properly join in on the girl talk?

"You have your café," he continues. "A musician will be traveling all the time. But someone who works at the studio on a more permanent basis."

He has a fair point. "But I'm just looking for a bit of fun." I say.

This time Flora and Sebastian are the ones to share the knowing glance. I roll my eyes at them, just because they've found their perfect mate doesn't mean that I will.

Chapter 10

Finnegan

Liliana takes the proffered glass of champagne and meets me in a cheers.

"It looks great! Thank you for putting it all together so quickly." I do mean it.

The party is well underway, but there's no sign of my mate yet. I worry that she won't be coming.

It's not something I can outright ask Sebastian or Flora. I don't even know if they are aware of my presence in Rosie's life yet.

Liliana's human mate chooses that moment to join us. The succubus pulls her against her, an arm snaking around her shoulders. They look so at ease with one another.

I wonder what it will feel like, having my mate pressed up against me, feeling completely blissed out in my presence. Will she even want that?

Not for the first time, I wonder if she will be into the same things as me. Not just in the bedroom, but also in every day life. Will she also want to spend her evenings working on business, way past the time that's proper?

Obviously, she is just as into her work as I am. There's no way that the passion I saw in her café just goes away after she shuts up shop for the evening. I could see her, meeting me at the studio after work and sitting with me while I finish up my meetings, doing her own thing.

Then we could get up to more than just *work* in my office...

The rich spicy scent of my mate wafts beneath my nose and my head snaps up, my gaze finding her instantly.

Her soft brown hair is in loose waves, pinned to one side with some sparkling clips. She's wearing a tight fitting dress that hugs her ample curves. It's a soft blue color and even from this distance I can see how it makes her bright eyes pop.

My legs move of their own accord, rushing across the space to greet her.

"Rosie!" Flora's chirpy voice calls out, cutting across my line of sight and pulling my mate into her arms.

Shit. What did I think I was doing?

I change direction, quickly moving to the bar off to the side. It's a good vantage point to watch their interaction.

Her scent is even more intense now that it's permeating the space. Pressing myself back against the bar, I resist the urge to go to her.

Oh how I wish I could throw her over my shoulder and take her somewhere private. Her long legs glow even in the dim lighting of the space, her hair catching the golden tones of the string lights strung up on the walls.

My pants resist against the pressure of my cock hardening in them. At least it is dark enough that my black pants should mask the sight. It's not something that I can help with her in that seductive dress. I need to feel her against me, to press my fingers into her plush body.

I can't though. Right now I need to find some way to build a relationship with her. Rosie wasn't just some woman that I found attractive and wanted to take to my bed. She was my mate. I needed to make sure that whatever foundation this is built on is built to last.

Chapter 11

R *osie*

I had planned to get ready for the party with Flora at her house. But disaster struck and one of my coffee machines broke down this afternoon. Luckily, I got a repair guy in to look at it but it took all evening.

Barely making it to the party on time was not on my agenda. I almost didn't want to go, but then I thought about how excited Flora was. Besides, was it weird that I wanted to see if the orc was here?

Flora found me right away when I arrived, pulling me aside to catch me up. She chats away, but I can't help my eyes from straying as they scan the room.

The telltale flash of Daisy's bright red hair catches the light, and I see her with her new mates, dancing and laughing. Cleo joins them while I watch, their giant kraken mate picking her up in his tentacles. My heart pangs with both joy and jealousy.

Do I want that?

"See anyone you like the look of?" Flora asks from my side.

I search the room some more, my gaze meeting the orc's, almost as if pulled by a magnet. Forcing my eyes to move, I carry on past his answering grin, pretending as though I didn't stare back at him for at least five seconds.

"Him." I say, gesturing to the next monster I see. I maybe regret that, the imposing male with the lower half of a snake noticing me staring.

"A naga? OK, go off, Rosie."

"Yeah, maybe that is a little advanced..." I nibble on my lip with nerves, but Flora just laughs it off.

"*Oh,*" she says. "One of the label execs is totally checking you out!"

A label exec? That sounds pretty fancy, whatever it means. I wonder what kind of monster would be an exec?

Maybe a sophisticated demon, like a succubus. Damn, a succubus sounds pretty good for a fun night.

"Where?" I ask, trying not to be obvious as Flora gestures to them.

"Don't look now, because he will totally see. He's the orc over by the bar."

The orc? Over by the bar?

Shit. Was that *my* orc? He had been leaning against the bar.

"Fancy watch? Sleek black suit?" I ask Flora, keeping my back to him.

"That's the one!" She clutches at my arm. "Ooh, had you checked him out already?! He's pretty handsome."

"Umm... kind of." I start to pull Flora down toward the door to the bathroom. "I need to catch you up on some things."

The pieces start to fit together. The fancy suits, the generous tip, knowing Flora's address to drop off the gift... He was a big shooter in the label and all the signs were right there.

I don't know what to think.

Slamming the door shut to the tiny space, I lock Flora into the bathroom stall with me.

"Whoa, babe." She runs a hand down my back. "What's up?"

"I kept something from you." I start. "Not on purpose really, or I mean, I wasn't planning on keeping it from you forever. It's just that I was happy to be spending time with you and catching up, and I didn't want to waste that time on speculating."

"Ro, it's all good." Flora's warm golden eyes meet mine, and I can see that she's not mad at me.

"OK." I take a deep breath. "The other day I was at your place, checking over everything. When *he* showed up."

"Finnegan?" She clarifies at my blank stare. "The orc. His name is Finnegan. He was at my house?"

"Yeah! But it wasn't weird, he was just dropping off a gift for you guys 'cause he thought you'd be back already." I toy with the ends of my hair. "Anyway, he was there and then the next day he showed up at my café."

"He *what*? In the human side of the city?"

I nod, unsure of what else to say.

"Well, did he do anything?"

"No! No, he just ate breakfast and left. He was pretty nice actually. Even left a giant tip for Ben because of the people who left."

A crease has formed between Flora's brows while she thinks over what I said.

"And he's been staring at you now, too..." She ponders aloud.

"Yeah, it is kind of weird." I shrug it off, though. "You know what? Maybe I'm overreacting. Let's go back out and have some fun! Who knows, maybe I will try things with the naga."

I open the stall before she can stop me, heading back into the party with Flora hot on my heels.

Chapter 12

Finnegan

Aspis has been speaking with my mate for far too long now.

I am aware on some level that some of the party goers have started to notice my staring. But I can't bear to look away as my naga colleague gets Rosie's full attention.

I want to say that Rosie has been acting strangely, then I remember that I know next to nothing about her. She had barely been at the party for a few minutes when Flora spotted me staring.

Rosie had dragged her into the bathroom and they were in there for a while. The whole time my eyes were stuck to the door, my senses cut off from her delicious scent. I was close to following her in there, my instincts taking over, when she finally stepped back out.

Rosie fled the bathroom, Flora close on her heels with concern on her face.

My mate had walked right past me, not sparing me a second glance as she walked toward Aspis with determination. Halfway there, Flora had given up her pursuit, giving me a surprisingly gentle smile, and making her way to some friends.

Did Flora know what was up? I'm almost certain that Rosie had caught her up on the events of the past few days now.

Aspis brushes a piece of fly away hair out of Rosie's face and I see red. I down my whiskey and order another, praying that I can keep my shit together and not walk over there.

I didn't really have any right to interrupt them. Rosie can do whatever she likes, I will certainly not be the one to try and control her.

My alpha instincts are at war with my logical mind. I know Aspis, he's a decent male. I also know that he has his eye on someone completely different, and that Rosie is probably of no interest to him at all.

But my gut doesn't believe that.

The one consolation is that Rosie's scent hasn't shifted. As far as I have learned, an omega's scent will shift slightly when they are turned on. Usually to a sweeter note.

Which means that Rosie isn't actually as into Aspis as it might seem.

Then why was she flirting with him? It made no sense. Unless... she wasn't trying to make me jealous, was she?

No, that's just me being self-centered. Rosie has given me no reason to believe that from our limited interactions.

Rosie leans into Aspis, her plush body pressing against his as she says something with a flirty smile.

That's enough.

"Hey, Rosie. I didn't know you were coming tonight." I am across the room with the words out of my mouth before I can even register the decision to do it. "Aspis." I say with a nod that is a clear dismissal.

He knows me well enough to excuse himself quickly. I am his boss, after all.

Rosie blinks up at me, confusion and petulance in her face. I know that I've ruined her fun, and now that I'm here I don't know what to say.

"Here, this is for you." Rosie holds out an envelope, and I can see the crisp hundred dollar bills poking out. "I appreciate the thought, but I can't take this."

I don't take the proffered envelope, instead searching her bright cerulean eyes. I hope she's not annoyed at me for it. But her gaze is soft and not at all annoyed.

"No, I want you to keep it. I know that I cleared out a lot of your customers."

Hesitating, Rosie stands there with the cash still held aloft. I gently clasp her hand and guide it back toward her purse.

Her skin is soft and supple, warmth seeping into my fingers. I hold her for longer than I should, until I eventually have to let go. Rosie's rich and decadent scent shifts to something sweeter, like a honey soaked strawberry bursting across my tongue.

"Why did you come to my café?" Her voice is barely a whisper of sound, my ears straining to hear. My gaze is stuck on her plump and glossy lips as I answer.

"I've heard great things about it." I've hunched over her body, blocking her from the view of the rest of the room. "And I wanted to see you again."

"Why?"

"Because I gave you a fright at the house, and that wasn't my intention." My hands itch to hold her, to feel her soft skin again. "I—"

"I have to go." Rosie cuts me off. I'm not even really sure as to what I was going to say.

My mate pulls back from me, not waiting for my response before she bolts.

Chapter 13

R *osie*

It's busy today, a line of people out onto the street.

My head is thumping, even though I barely took a sip of my drink last night. I cringe again, thinking about how I ran away from Finnegan. I'm still not entirely sure why.

I was into him, the way he crouched over me made me feel protected. He looked at me like he could see straight through to my soul. It was somehow electrifying and unnerving at the same time.

My pussy is growing wet again just thinking about it. About him.

That's why I ran, if I'm being honest with myself. I had been looking for some flirty fun, not the intensity of his gaze, the serious way that he looked at me. Like I was the only person at the party, he had stared only at me.

That should be creepy, right?

There's just something about how he gave me his full focus that must have done it for me, in some strange way.

Shaking my head, I get back to work. I'm glad that it's busy, I can focus on taking orders and getting the line moving along. My brain will be too busy to think about Finnegan.

The line for takeout is finally fully inside, some of the tables emptying out, when I catch my first glance of green.

Shit. Is he really here right *now*? Like, give me some breathing room, dude.

A couple customers leave the line as he enters the café, choosing to leave rather than be near him. I want to be mad, but he should be allowed to come here if he wants to.

Saving myself any further embarrassment from last night, I have Ben serve him, his sandy blond hair fluttering in the breeze of the door as another customer leaves.

It's fine. I'm fine.

I pointedly ignore him, busying myself with serving the customers that we still have. Ben can serve him. Finnegan can have his lunch and enjoy the café without having to interact with me.

The plan was to ignore him, and yet my eyes find his more than once. My mind drifts to last night again, now that I don't have the distraction of all the customers. I had thought his eyes were black, but when we were close last night I realized that they were the darkest shade of green. A rich, plant green, like one of the begonias on the back shelf. They're beautiful.

I tell Farrow that I'm taking a break, heading up to my apartment for a bit. Hopefully he'll be gone by the time I get back.

Chapter 14

Finnegan

I keep going to her café, even though she ignores me.

I'm not sure what I did at the party, but she's created a distance between us that I can't seem to penetrate.

Not that I've tried overly hard, I think that patience is key in this case. Pushing her the other night clearly didn't help matters.

She pretends as though she wants nothing to do with me. But I catch her looking at me often, and her scent sweetens when I am around.

Either way, I am content to sit and watch my mate working. I can tell how passionate she is about her café, how happy it makes her. When I don't catch her watching me, I see her in her element.

She's beautiful. The soft pink of her apron always making those gorgeous eyes pop. Strands of her hair falling out of a messy bun on her head more often than not. I want to be there, behind the counter with her, tucking those pieces behind her ears.

Today was no different until now. But I can see my avocado toast sitting on the window ledge of the kitchen. I haven't brought myself to try anything else, knowing that this is what Rosie served me that first day. Ben is busy with another customer, so her usual fall guy is occupied.

I watch her as she realizes the situation. I wonder if she will send Farrow, or if I will finally get an opportunity to speak with my mate.

Rosie picks it up and makes her way towards me. Her scent is overwhelming in the best way possible. I haven't been this close to her since the party.

"Enjoy your meal!" She chirps, neatly placing the plate in front of me and running away promptly.

Fuck. I was so enamored by her presence that I didn't even get the chance to convince her to speak with me.

Chapter 15

R*osie*

It's been four days.

Four days of him coming to my café for lunch, and four days of me doing my best to avoid him.

Yesterday I had a slip up. Ben had been taking an order from an older couple who were struggling to read the menu. He was spending ages helping them to decide on their order. Farrow is still nervous around the orc, so it was up to me to serve Finnegan.

I didn't give him a moment to say much, just dropped off his plate and told him to enjoy. Every day he gets the same avocado toast, and I almost want to encourage him to try something else. But I hold back, trying to keep some distance.

If I don't encourage him, maybe he'll get sick of trying. Then I'll have my café to myself again. Not to mention my regular customers back in the door.

Flora says that if he is making me uncomfortable, I should just tell him. She insists that he's a nice guy though. At the label, he's seen as strict but fair, but I disagree.

I wouldn't call him strict at all.

Whenever Finnegan catches me looking at him, he gives me a warm smile. Even his teeth and tusks seem normal now.

I still don't understand why he keeps coming here though. It's affecting my business and I need to do something about it.

Flora's suggestion seems a bit brazen, but maybe I could just talk to him. I had initially avoided it because I felt awkward after the party, but the longer I keep this up the more likely that this is what I'm embarrassed about.

The café is busy this morning, and it takes me a while to realize that the time Finnegan usually drops by has come and gone. A pang permeates my chest as disappointment flows through me. Is he not coming today?

But I was going to talk to him. I was going to serve him and try to find out why he was coming here.

Maybe my tactics had worked, maybe ignoring him for a few days was all it took.

I busy myself behind the counter, using a quiet moment to organize some extra cups and napkins in the cupboards. I can't see the door from this position, but when I pop back up again the biggest smile spreads across my face.

A warm feeling envelopes me as Finnegan walks through the door.

Maybe I don't mind him being here after all.

Deciding to be brave, I take a deep breath and bring him a menu. He has his own spot at this point, a seat by the window where he can sit in the stream of sunlight. It makes his green skin glow, and gives a shining effect to his tusks.

"Hi Fin," The nickname falls from my mouth as I hand him the menu card. "You have to try something different today. There's plenty on the menu."

Finnegan looks dumbfounded at me, standing before him and talking. I have to laugh a little at his expression. It doesn't take him too long though, a gorgeous smile blooming in return and nearly knocking me off my feet.

"Well, what am I trying today then?" He passes me the menu back, reminding me of our game from his first visit.

"Sweet or savory?"

He almost seems to sniff the air before answering, "sweet."

I nod, heading back to the kitchen to place his order.

Once Finnegan has finished his plate of pancakes loaded with berries, honey, and clotted cream, I come by to see what he thought.

Tossing my towel over my shoulder, I pull out the chair across from him and sit down.

"What did you think?" I ask, desperately trying not to be affected by his charming grin.

"Delicious." His tongue darts out to lick his lip. It's *black*.

We don't speak for a moment, and I take the opportunity to really look at him. His hair is a bit more relaxed today, the ends at his nape. Not for the first time, I wonder what it would be like to run my hands through the glossy strands. I'm even jealous of the volume he seems to manage at the root, almost covering the pointed tips of his ears, mine could never.

His face is strong, high cheekbones and a broad jawline. Thick black lashes frame his green eyes, which look even brighter in the sunlight now.

I'd feel weird about staring if he wasn't also doing the same. I wonder what he sees when he looks at me. I must look so boring to someone like him, surrounded by unique and interesting monsters.

"Why are you here?" I say on a breathy sigh. "Why do you keep coming to my café?"

I expect him to say it's for the food, or to lie about it.

"For business," he says, instead. "I've been thinking about making you an offer. To invest."

That's... not what I expected. I take a second to process, not sure how to behave.

"I—" Do I entertain this? "I'm not so sure I need any investing, if I'm being honest. I'm happy with the way the café is, and I own the building outright."

Finnegan grins at that, an almost proud look on his face. Why would he be proud of me?

"I find that hard to believe, Rosie." The sound of my name in his mouth is far too nice to hear. I need to focus right now. "Someone like you, who has built this from the ground up in such a short time... Can you honestly tell me that you're satisfied? That you don't feel the itch to do more, now that you have what you wanted?"

It's almost scary, how well he understands the thoughts I have been having lately. I don't admit it aloud, but he's right.

"Hear me out, at least." He continues. How did I ever think that his eyes were black? I can't deny the warmth there, the vulnerability.

"Come back tomorrow with a proposal then." I say, standing up and getting back to work, taking his plate with me.

Chapter 16

Rosie

When Finnegan comes into the café today, he walks right up to me at the counter. He has some file folders in his hand, and he looks like he means business.

"Do you want to do this out here, or do you have an office?" He asks, getting straight to the point. I kind of like seeing him in business mode, being assertive like this. A flutter starts in my stomach as I look him over.

"Sort of," I giggle. "Come upstairs."

He follows me through the storage room in the back of the café and up my stairwell.

"Is this where you live?" He asks, as I lead him through my door and into the kitchen.

"Yeah," I realize now that I maybe shouldn't have taken the strange male up into my private space alone. But there's something about him that makes me feel safe enough to trust him.

"Coffee or tea?" I ask, gesturing for him to sit at the table while I move into the open plan kitchen area. He eyes the wall of tea ingredients, shelves of different dried flowers, herbs and fruit.

"Tea, please. Whatever you recommend."

I get to work on a quick custom blend for him, thinking about his sweet tooth when doing so.

Once I have a pot brewing, I set it on the table with two cups. He's been unabashedly looking around from his seat while he waits. I wonder what he must think of my colorful apartment.

"So, big guy. Tell me what you're thinking." I mean about the investment proposal, but do wish I could know what's going on in his head in general.

"I want to preface this by saying that if you want to make any changes or have any other ideas yourself, that this is a totally open platform. Even if you decide all you want from me is some no strings attached business advice."

I nod as I pour us two cups of tea. "OK, I hear you."

Finnegan gives me a firm nod.

"I'm thinking an expansion from a unit perspective. Opening multiple locations, essentially. It could be a slower process, working with designers to match the branding exactly, taking the time to hire staff that are the perfect culture fit.

"I really think what you have here is special, Rosie. Did you know that humans bring takeout from your café to the studio? It's how I knew about this place.

"I would propose the first new location to be in the general area of the studio for that reason. I'd love to have an in-house branch in the studio itself, but I don't think that would be as good of a prospect from a revenue perspective."

"Wait," I try to keep up. "So you want to open a second location of my café next to the studio?"

"Yes, I think it's a prime location in an up and coming area, with people who have already bought into your brand."

"Huh," I didn't realize that so many monsters liked my drinks. "Having a location near Flora's house would be fun too."

But that would mean I would be stepping away from this one at least some of the time. Who would manage it? Would I be managing two locations at once? That's probably too much to expect of myself.

I didn't think that I'd ever want to expand in this way. But then again, what other way was there for me to grow the business? And it's not like I had that kind of money anyway. Well, not without Finnegan's help at least.

"How would the investment work?" He can't help a small smile at my question, and it makes me want to please him more. But I need to keep things professional right now.

"I pay the initial investment. If things go well, I would ask for 10% of profits until the investment is repaid."

"That's not an investment..." I try to explain but I can see it in his eyes that he knows what I am about to say, so I switch gears. "Why do you want to help me?"

"I told you already, Rosie." His hand closes over mine where it sits on the table next to my cup, the warmth seeping into me and sending a tingle down my spine. "I think you have something special here. I want everyone to be able to access that."

Is he really just being a nice person? He seems genuine.

"Can I share a copy of this with my lawyer to look over?" I want to make sure I'm not missing something here.

"Of course."

Chapter 17

Rosie sits across from me as we sip on our tea. I'm trying not to show on my face how proud I am of her. That she wants to bring these papers by her lawyer is the smartest move.

I'm also trying not to freak out that I'm in her apartment and we are just casually chatting.

"So, we'd be business partners, huh?" She asks, her eyes lit up with excitement.

I hadn't planned on expanding Rosie's café until after the party, when I came back again and focused on the whole establishment rather than just her.

Not a single thing I've said to her has been a lie. I truly believe that she has something special here, and I would want to invest in this business regardless.

However, I would never expect profits from my mate. So I worked that into my plan. She can run it all by her lawyer, but he will only tell her that I am a fool. If she doesn't earn back the money, I am at a loss, and if she does, I only break even. She was right when she said it wasn't an investment at all.

"I wouldn't say partners," I chuckle. "It's more that you will tell me what you want to do, and I will pay for it. But the decisions are all up to you. Not that I won't be giving any advice I think you need."

Her warm smile lights up my soul. Her coloring compliments the butter yellow walls behind her. In fact, her whole apartment is a chromatic wonderland.

I wonder what she'd think of my house. It's modern and pretty basic in its coloring. She would make it so much more alive if she were to leave her mark. I can almost imagine what changes she'd make, what sort of furniture she would buy. If I'm being honest with myself, I've left my house pretty bare boned so that whenever I found my mate they would be able to put their stamp on it.

It's easy. Sitting here and speaking with my mate over the tea she brewed. I compliment her on the blend, impressed that she can whip something up that quickly.

"It's all practice," she insists. But I know a talent when I see it.

My phone dings, a message from Aspis on an ongoing copyright case. It's not urgent, but it does remind me of the time.

"I better get back to work." I say, placing my copies of the contracts away in my folder.

"I thought you were the boss." Rosie says with a wink. But she picks up our cups, bringing them to her sink.

I follow her on instinct, not really thinking about the small space. When she turns around, I'm nearly on top of her.

"In work, yes, I'm mostly the boss." I say, moving myself closer so that we're a hair's width apart. Inhaling her scent this close nearly makes me lose all control. "But sometimes I prefer to not be. Sometimes I want to be told what to do."

Rosie's eyes widen, her pupils dilating, and her scent sweetening. Fuck, I hope she's as into that as she seems.

"I feel the same." Her voice takes on a huskier quality. "Sometimes I like to follow a strong command." She trails a finger up my arm slowly, "but more often than not, I like to take charge."

I swallow to prevent myself from making a whimpering sound. Her eyes track the movement, her little pink tongue darting out to lick her lips.

"But right now," she points her finger to my chest. "You have to get back to work."

Chapter 18

Rosie

After Finnegan insists that I don't need to walk him out, I shut the door firmly behind him.

Fuck.

I don't know whether I need to go to my bedroom right now to masturbate or call Flora to catch her up on everything. My mind should be focused on his business plan and the investment, and I really need to book in a meeting with my lawyer.

But holy shit, I think I'm into Finnegan. Like, really into Finnegan.

Girl talk. I need girl talk like right now.

"Hey, babe." Flora answers on the second ring. My beautiful, reliable best friend.

"Oh my God, Flora." I gush.

"Ooh, give me the tea! What happened?" She knows immediately by my tone that I've called her with something juicy. It's just a little weird that it's about me.

"I like him." I say, placing the phone on my counter and switching it to speaker as I pace.

"Who?" Flora whispers, her voice lined with curiosity.

"Finnegan, of course! Who else?"

"Well, the last time we spoke about it, you didn't seem very pleased that I caught him watching you." I roll my eyes, she knew exactly who I was talking about.

"But this is good!" Flora continues. "Because he *was* into you. So you could totally go there. He's super hot, too!"

"It's not that simple." I cover my face with my hands. "He just offered to invest in my brand and to help me open a new branch of the café near the studio."

"Oh, shit." Flora squeals. "That's so exciting!"

"No, you don't get it." I'm getting a bit frustrated with her happy responses. "He wants to go into business with me, not into *bed*. And besides, I shouldn't be mixing business with pleasure, right?"

Flora stays quiet for a minute before she speaks. "Maybe he's investing *because* he likes you. Or at least, it might have a little something to do with it. And Rosie, girl, I'm the last person to speak to about the downsides of mixing business and pleasure. I love how much time it means me and Sebastian get to spend together."

"That's just because you're mates." I say, sounding like a petulant child. "For all my luck, Finnegan will probably find his own mate and leave me hanging. And then I'll have to sit by and watch them while we work on my café together."

"Rosie, can I be real with you right now?"

"No." I sigh, rubbing at my eyes some more. "Yes."

"You're being ridiculous. All I'm seeing is that you like him, he likes you, and he's investing in your business. These are all really good things. You should be happy."

I know she's right, on a logical level. But everything is happening all at once and I have no idea how to process it.

Should I keep things professional with Finnegan, or should I make a move? Is that even a question? I couldn't keep my hands to myself earlier, and I was trying.

Chapter 19

Rosie

I drink nearly half of my cup of tea before I pick up the papers again.

There it is, held on by a paper clip on the first page. His personal phone number, or at least I think so. The actual documents themselves have a completely different line listed under his information.

I snuggle in under my pink and white checkered throw blanket with my tea, unsure of what to do. What would I even say?

My lawyer looked through the papers yesterday and gave them the all clear. Finnegan was right, because he did remark that this wasn't a good deal for the investor. My lawyer even said that Finnegan would end up losing money from it.

Thinking back over what Flora said, I wonder if she's correct. Is Finnegan doing this because he likes me?

I could sit back and be flattered, but then that means there is so much pressure on me to give him a chance. I'm not even sure he really likes me though! Sure, we've had a few intense moments, but I could be reading those wrong.

I haven't heard from him since our moment in my kitchen. Thinking back to what he said, I can't believe my luck. From what he had said, it sounds like he's just like me, wanting to take control at times and not at others. I wonder what it would feel like, to have him submit to me, this hulking orc.

Shifting in my seat, I try not to think about the wetness pooling in my panties at the thought. I need to focus. Picking up my phone, I type in the number, my finger hovering over the call button.

OK, I can do this.

"Hello?" He answers after barely less than a ring.

"Hi." I hesitate. "Is that Finnegan?"

God, what is wrong with me? Of course it's him. As if I couldn't recognize the deep timbre of his voice anywhere.

"Hi, Rosie." I hear a shuffle, almost like he's walking around. "How are you?"

"Oh, uh... I'm good." I was kind of expecting him to get down to business right away. "How are you?"

"Great, now that you've called." Does he really mean that? "I was hoping you would. I didn't have a number to reach you on, and work has been too busy for me to make it down to the café the past couple days."

It strikes me, all of a sudden, how inconvenient it is for Finnegan to be coming here as regularly as he was, especially in the middle of the work day. I'm sure he's a busy guy as well. I still don't really know what it is he does for his job, but it's definitely important and therefore time consuming.

"I had wanted to ask you out to lunch." He continues at my silence. "Tomorrow. If you can make that."

"Oh! Yeah, that makes sense." I hadn't thought about it, but the signing of the contracts and stuff will need to be in person. And he probably wants to talk to me about the finer details, or start to plan. "I spoke with my lawyer and I'm happy to talk some more about it all. Tomorrow is perfect, I can get Farrow to take over the café. Honestly, it will be good practice for her if I'll be splitting my time between two locations more often. You know, I should properly introduce you to her."

Oh, God. I stop speaking abruptly, realizing the word vomit train I was going down.

"Yeah, we can talk about the investment." Finnegan has a layer of disappointment in his voice, but I can't understand why. "I'll text you the address."

He says goodbye quickly, and I'm left to ponder what changed. He had been excited that I called initially...

Holy shit. He hadn't asked me to meet to talk business, had he?

Had Finnegan just asked me out on a date? Did I make it into a business meeting?

Well, fuck.

Chapter 20

Finnegan

The small restaurant was happy to accommodate my last minute reservation, surprisingly. I know that they've been super busy, being the only place to get food in this part of town.

A whiff of red wine hits my nose before I spot her. Rosie shines, dressed in a burgundy silk blouse and dark wash flare jeans that hug her thighs. The look shows off her ample curves, and I need to stop myself from drooling.

I had wanted to take her out on a proper date. After our moment in her apartment, I thought that maybe things were going in the right direction. That maybe she was starting to let herself see this as *more*. Her scent had been shifting to that delicious, sweet fruitiness nearly all the time, and it emboldened me to say something suggestive. And her response had been tantalizing.

Which is why I thought that it would finally be appropriate to ask her on a date. That maybe she was finally ready for that.

Of course she saw it as a follow up to our business discussion.

I had been planning on trying to woo her. Getting a car to pick her up and take her to a nice, upscale restaurant for lunch. There was a perfect spot that I had in mind, knowing Rosie's adventurous palate and how she would love to eat from the best chefs. In the end it felt inappropriate to take her somewhere like that when she made it clear that she only wanted to talk business.

I haven't given up on my mate, though. I was just going to have to be more subtle about it all.

Waving at her from our table, I stand up to help her into her seat. "You look beautiful," I say, leaning in to subtly sniff her as I pull out her chair.

"Oh, thank you." She is flustered, her cheeks rosy as she settles in. "So do you."

A laugh busts out of me. "I don't get called beautiful very often."

We're in the general area of the studio, and so there is a mix of monsters and humans surrounding us. I would think that Rosie would be more interested in any of the newer types of monsters that she hasn't seen before. In particular, there was a rare crystal gargoyle in the corner whom I'm sure she's never seen before. But no, she only has eyes for me.

Chapter 21

R^{osie}

I'm trying, desperately trying, to focus on the business things that Finnegan is saying.

Every time he smiles, or shifts in his seat, I'm distracted by how hot he looks. He wears a black suit with a white shirt unbuttoned a little at the top, the crisp lines standing out against his skin. It's not the first time I've seen him in this look, but it feels different today, I just can't put my finger on why.

The place we're at has an interesting clientele. A mix of humans and monsters all come in, no one really batting an eye at that. It's so different to when Finnegan comes to my café, and again I wonder why he would put himself through that. Why he would face that prejudice just to make an investment that isn't even going to make him any money? I don't want to push it with him, in case he realizes how bad a deal it is and walks out. But maybe Flora was right... maybe he is into me.

"How's your food?" Finnegan asks, a small smirk on his face.

"Not great," I admit. Why does he look kind of happy about that?

"Yeah, we could really do with a better place to eat in this area, don't you think? Maybe a nice café..."

Oh. He did not.

"Did you take me here to prove that it was bad?" He's trying to hold in a chuckle at my realization. I poke his arm, "Fin! Oh my God, you can't do that!"

"Why not? I had a point to prove."

The glint in his eye as he teases me is unbelievably sexy. Fuck, his whole person is unbelievably sexy.

"Fine." I look him in the eyes as I speak, to communicate my seriousness. "I'll do it."

"You'll do what?" There's a glimmer of hope in his eyes, his brow softening to give them a rounded look.

"I'll go into business with you. Open the café in this part of town, take your business advice, the whole nine yards."

His hand clasps mine on the table, giving me a reassuring squeeze. "You won't regret it."

"I'll even sign the contracts now if you want."

We go through the documents together, Finnegan wearing a huge smile the whole time. It's kind of adorable, this huge male happy that I want to take his money.

He lets me know that he will start looking into potential locations and property, and that I'll hear from him once he has a few viewings lined up. I hope it doesn't take him too long. If the past few days were anything to go by, his daily visits to my café were long over, and I missed having him around.

He walks me to my car after our mediocre meal, being much more open on how we felt about the food now that we were outside. It's fun, critiquing it with him, and I tell him about how I like to eat out when I can and be an internal critic.

Instead of shaking my hand in a goodbye, Finnegan leans forward, pressing a gentle kiss to my cheek. His tusk brushes against my ear in a teasing tickle that sends a shiver to my toes.

Chapter 22

R *osie*

It's been a week since I went for lunch with Finnegan. A week of touching my cheek and remembering him kissing me there. A week of torturing myself, wondering when I'm going to hear from him next.

Why can't he be as forward and intense as he was in the first place? I'd give anything to get him to come into my café today, I wouldn't even make him try something new.

I don't really know when it fully shifted, but I really like him.

God, I feel like a horny teenager again. I feel like I'm going crazy.

I call Flora, putting her on speaker as I make my tea. Maybe she'd like to hang out today or something. Anything to get my mind off *him*.

"Oh, Flora," I say when she answers. "I can't do this anymore. Maybe I should text him? He didn't say he didn't want to hear from me, just that he'd be in touch when he had somewhere to show me."

"Yeah, of course you can text him." Flora says again, ever the patient friend. This is the fifth time we've had this conversation. "But why don't we work on what you're going to say. I don't think you should just text him if you don't know what your intentions are. These monster guys are pretty intense, so just be aware of that."

"Ugh, that's my problem!" I sigh, pressing my forehead against my fridge door in exasperation. "I didn't think I wanted anything serious, so I pushed him away when he first showed interest. And now I'm wondering why I ever thought that. Not to mention that I've clearly been shoving him into some sort of 'business zone' after our last couple interactions."

"I know, girl. I get it, trust me." She's not wrong there. Flora had neatly packed Sebastian away into the 'grumpy guy that I work with' box when she first started to get feelings for him. "But I think you need to make a move. Show him that you're not just interested in business."

"But how do I—"

My phone starts to buzz, alerting me of another person attempting to call me.

"Shit, Flora. He's calling me right now!"

"Then *answer*." She hangs up our call and my phone switches to ringing loudly. My fingers fumble as I hit the answer button.

"Hi, Rosie." His voice is just as buttery soft and deep as I remember. "How are you?"

"Hey," I take a quick breath, trying to calm my nerves. "Long time no speak, I've missed you around the café."

Great. Way to come off desperate.

"Me too." He chuckles a little but I can hear that he genuinely means it. "I was hoping you might be free today? I have something to show you."

"Is it a property?!" I can't help the excitement in my voice. A whole new space to design from scratch. We'll be keeping the same color scheme and branding, but the layout will be different in every location.

"Why don't you come and find out?"

"Text me the address! I'll be there in thirty minutes."

Chapter 23

Finnegan

Rosie's tiny red car pulls up to the address, easily parking outside on the quiet street.

I'm nervous to see her. It has been a horrible, pain-filled week. I almost texted her so many times, my phone in my hand with the message typed before I deleted it.

My consensus was that I had been coming off too strong initially. Showing up to her café and basically stalking her like that. But I did say that I would reach out when I had some property viewings lined up, so I needed to stick to that.

I had already envisioned the café on this street, in this new strip of premises. It's about a ten minute walk from the studio, and there's plenty of parking along the street. It's perfect.

When I told Rosie that I'd be in touch once I had a viewing set up, I didn't think that it would take this long. Margo, the developer of the street, took this long to reply to me. I even had my assistant, Cynthia, reach out too.

So yes, this week has been a disaster.

The lunch was great, though. And I was even brave enough to give her a kiss on the cheek as we said goodbye. My lips had tasted of her afterwards, the rich heady flavor on the tip of my tongue. I needed more of her, this waiting was torture.

I liked to think of myself as a patient guy, but watching Rosie get out of that car right now was testing my patience.

It's a crisp fall day, but my mate wears a short little skirt that stops high above her knees. Her legs are bare, ending in a pair of heeled boots. She waves at me before bending to grab her purse from the car, showing me a scandalous glance up her skirt.

Fuck. I fist my hands at my side and wait by the door to the potential café. Is she teasing me on purpose? Because I was not going to last very long without touching her if that was the case.

"Hey, Fin!" She walks right up to me, placing her hands on my chest and pulling me down. It takes a moment for me to realize that she's kissing my cheek in greeting. Once I catch on, the movement is smooth and successful.

I haven't exactly thought about the logistics of all of this too much just yet. But Rosie was significantly shorter than me. When I straighten up, her eyes are level with the top of my abs.

She's buzzing with excitement, trying to look around me and into the window of the empty building.

"Hang on." I tease, stepping in her line of sight. "Let me set it all up for you."

"Fine," she sighs dramatically, but her cute smile shines through.

"It's a new development, obviously. Hence why the street is so empty right now. I know the developer, Margo, and we should be able to get a decent price on it. The studio is only a few minutes drive that way, and—you know what, yes. Let's just look inside."

I couldn't help myself, seeing her eyes zone out.

"I trust you. The location is probably perfect." She walks around me, opening the door to the space. My chest puffs up with pride at her admission of trust. "Come on!"

I follow her inside, watching as she takes in the concrete space. It's blank, the plumbing pipes and electrical wires all visible on the walls. It doesn't look like much to me, but I know that with her eye for design, Rosie will know if it's any good.

"It's perfect!" She squeals, after a minute.

Rosie grips my arm, holding me close as she points to the different areas and what she thinks would look good where. It's a bit bigger than her current location, and she explains that she can do some more interesting seating arrangements.

She keeps a hold of me the whole time, and I try not to freak out at having her so close.

Chapter 24

Rosie

This place is amazing. There's so much potential, and I can really let my creativity free.

I don't know why I was worried that it would end up being a carbon copy of my first café, but it's going to have a completely different layout. I've already started to tell Finnegan about it all, walking him through the space with me as I explain.

He listens intently, even adding in his own opinions here and there.

Eventually, I let go of his arm and head into the back room to take a look around.

They seem to be further along in the construction here. The walls are lined with built in shelves, and there's a door that leads into a small utility space, counters already fitted.

"Fin! Oh!" I turn, belatedly realizing that he is right behind me in the tiny space. "Sorry, I didn't mean to shout in your face."

He keeps moving towards me, boxing me in against the counter and craning my neck to see his face. My gaze meets his dark green in the fluorescents and I freeze.

"Rosie..." His voice trails off, unsure.

My gaze flicks to his lips and the tusks there. What would it be like to kiss him? Would they be a hindrance? Or would the scrape of them against my skin feel good?

He's dressed much more casual today, a navy blue sweater and jeans, his hair relaxed and free of product. I've been thinking about how it would feel to run my hands through his hair and fist those thick strands. My hands reach up of their own accord, settling on his chest, well above my head. The fabric is softer than I expected.

Finnegan crouches over me, leaning forward with his hands caging me in against the counter. He sniffs the air above my head, and while you would think that is weird, it actually feels comforting. Pressing my head against his chest, I breathe him in too.

His smell is comforting, a hint of a blossom, maybe some rosehip. It's like a yummy tea that I would make for myself.

"Can I...?" I lean back at his words, searching his face. "I want to kiss you."

Finally.

"Yes." The word is breathy, and I realize how quiet the room feels.

Finnegan's hands shift from the counter and onto my hips, lifting me up onto the high shelf. Our heads are almost level, and I feel tiny against him. My legs slot between his and they press tightly to secure his grip.

My hands are so small against his face, which is so much larger than any human man that I've been with. His skin is tougher than I expected too, like a very supple leather. Tracing his cheekbone, my fingers brush against his tusk, a smooth ivory against my skin.

"They won't hurt you." He says, shifting them beneath my hands.

"I didn't think that they would." I move to cup his jaw again. "I just wanted to know what they felt like."

Using my new found purchase, I pull his face closer to mine and press my lips against his. A tingle winds its way through me as heat pools in my core.

The tusks aren't strange at all, they hardly touch my face at this angle. My hands finally sink into his hair and pull him even closer. Taking control of our kiss, I slip my tongue into his mouth, deepening it and pressing myself against him more. He's like putty against me, so eager to submit. He keeps a death grip on one of my hips, his other hand submerging in my hair and stroking against my scalp.

Something stiff pushes against my thigh from the top. There's no way... Freeing one of my hands from his tangle of hair, I reach down to feel. Finnegan hisses in my mouth as my hand grips his cock as it strains through the fabric of his jeans against his *leg*.

Holy shit.

Palming his girthy cock, I grip his hair even tighter as I focus on kissing him again. Having the control like this with a huge Monster is intoxicating and goes right to my head.

"Fuck, Rosie." Finnegan breaks our kiss, his breath heavy and panting.

He grips my waist, picking me up off the counter and against him. A dark blush has formed across his cheeks, his hair mussed from my attentions. He kicks the door shut, straightening up to his full height as he presses my back against the hard wood.

My legs wrap around his waist, my hands fisted in his sweater. Finnegan is done playing the submissive, he ravishes me. His lips find my neck as his hands slip up my skirt and cup my bare ass underneath.

Soft moans escape me as I writhe against him, careful of his tusks scraping against me in a dangerous thrill.

"You smell so fucking good," he groans into my neck. His tongue darts out to taste me with his kisses. My pussy has to be soaking wet, the friction of his body against it is too good to stop my movement.

I barely manage a groan in response, my head tipped back to bear my neck even more. He palms my ass, almost doing the grinding for me. Shit, I think I could cum like this. But that would be way too embarrassing.

Tugging on his hair pointedly gets him to move away from my neck. I kiss him again, but this time slowing us down a little and easing the tension until it's only gentle pecks.

"So... I really love the property." I say, when we fully break away.

Finnegan presses his forehead against mine as he laughs, relaxing into me.

"I'm taking you on a date." He tells me, his voice pure assertion.

"I'm taking you on a date." He tells me, his voice pure assertion.

Chapter 25

F*innegan*

For the past two days, all I have been able to think about is that kiss. It replays in my mind like a movie.

Rosie gripping my cock through my jeans, her body pressed flush between me and the wall. I've been perpetually hard since then, nothing granting me release. I'm a little ashamed to say that I probably would have fucked her in that utility room if she hadn't slowed me down. She was right to, though. She deserves to be wined and dined before we have sex for the first time. I also want her to be comfortable, and there was nothing comfortable about that utility room.

Today is the day that I get to see her again. After our kiss, I made sure that we had plans. Once she had gotten on the road again, I called Cynthia to get us booked in to one of the nicest restaurants on the monster side of town. I just know that Rosie will love the food there.

Straightening my tie in the mirror one more time, I take a last look at myself. I look happier, much more so than I ever have. Hopefully, I will still look as happy after tonight. It's time that I tell Rosie that we're mates. I don't think it's wise to keep it to myself any longer and I hate feeling like I am lying to her.

I head out to the car idling in the drive. The driver makes quick work of the trip to Rosie's café. She's waiting out back at the private entrance to her apartment when I arrive. The driver opens the door for her and she easily steps inside the enormous vehicle. Sometimes I forget how small she really is.

My mate shines in a satin gold dress this evening, with matching strappy heels ending off her glowing legs.

"You're stunning." I say by way of greeting.

"You're not so bad yourself." She says with a wink.

Rosie slots into the seat next to me, setting her folded shawl and purse down before giving me her full attention. She rests her hand on my thigh for purchase as she stretches up to kiss me on the cheek.

"Ooh, we match!" She toys with my tie. I glance down to see that she's correct, thin gold thread outlines a pattern on the wine red fabric.

We chat for most of the drive to the restaurant, always touching in some way. Rosie is full of flirty quips, and I feel like I'm really getting an insight into her unfiltered personality now.

I love it.

We're shown to an alcove table when we get to the restaurant. It's easy for us to watch the patrons but their eyes aren't drawn to us. Everyone is too interested in themselves to really notice the tiny human next to me.

We sit next to one another on the curved bench seat, Rosie keeping a hand on my thigh as we wait for our orders.

"So what got you into the music industry?" She asks, turning to face me fully.

"My dad was a musician," I explain. "A pretty famous one, by orc standards. Except none of my brothers were interested in music like I was. I'm a decent amateur musician, which gives me enough knowhow to make the decisions I need to for my job. But my real passion has always been business, and seeing the potential in others."

"I'm almost embarrassed to ask at this point, but what *is* your job? Flora said you were an exec at the label, but I've got to be honest, I have no idea what that means." She runs her fingers through her soft golden brown waves, pushing them to one side.

I can't help but chuckle, resting my arm on the back of the seat and brushing my fingers gently over her freshly bared shoulder.

"I'm the Director of Label Strategy." Her brow furrows a little, and I realize that I'm going to need to provide further explanation. "It's kind of exactly what it sounds like. I'm the person who decides on any big decisions we have on strategy, all business or marketing related. It's not entirely on my own, there's a whole host of people involved with the research and discussion, but ultimately it's my guidance that they follow.

"It was my idea that we merge the human and monster markets, for example."

Her mouth opens on an 'o', pretty little teeth showing through.

"I didn't realize you were *that* important." She looks a little nervous all of a sudden, and I hold her shoulder in place in case she decides to bolt.

"It's just a job, Rosie." My thumb strokes her and she gives my leg a little squeeze.

"Yeah, you're right. Sorry," she laughs at herself, "my best friend is literally a famous singer. I obviously keep good company."

"What about you?" I ask, shifting the subject. "Why a coffee shop?"

"Oh, that one's easy! I just love food so much, and designing menus. I like to cook, and I'm not bad at it, but I never really wanted to work in a kitchen. My other passion is one you have seen too,"

"Making tea." I finish for her.

"Yep! I love coming up with different recipes for different people or for different moods. So a proper dinner restaurant was out of the question." She looks around us, lost in her head for a moment, but I wait to let her finish. "I like having company too. Running a café is never lonely. There's always someone there, even if they're just studying quietly on their own, you feel like you're a part of that. It's a safe haven for others. I wanted to make a space that was relaxing and welcoming for anyone."

"Even an orc who scares away half your customers." I tease, understanding my mate on a much deeper level.

"Even then." She agrees. "Although I'm glad how that one has worked out for me so far."

My heart warms at her admission.

Our first course is served and with it the topic of conversation. I've made sure to sign us up for the full chef's tasting menu with matching wines.

We spend the evening discussing the flavors and pairings. Rosie is a connoisseur, filled to the brim with different knowledge on it all. She explains that she majored in food science in university and that's where her love for food really began.

"It's funny, I love all these complicated, complex dishes and flavor combinations. But it's the simple, basic meals that I come back to time and time again. This is all lovely for a treat, but when I went to design my own menu I wanted to just make the basics with a fun twist."

"I can see that in your menus." I say, stroking her hand in my lap as we finish the last of our wine. "They're all modern classics with a hint of something different or a clever change."

"I've never once seen you read my menu!" She jokingly smacks my arm.

"Do you think I signed up to invest in your café without reading your menu?" I chuckle at her naivety. "I studied it. Even tried to recreate some of it at home using the images on your website as a guide."

"But..." She shakes her head. "Why did you always make me pick for you?"

"Because I wanted what *you* liked best. I was there to see you, Rosie, don't be fooled by all my fanfare. I wanted to eat your favorite foods and be in your company while you got used to being near anoOrc.

"I wanted to ask you out that first day in Sebastian and Flora's house. But I had just given you such a fright, and I wasn't sure how you would feel about being with a monster."

"Oh," she says, simply. But I can tell that she's processing all that information.

The waiter chooses that moment to come by with the check, and I quickly pay for the meal so that we can have some privacy.

"Thank you," she says for probably the fourth time. "I don't often get to go out to meals like this."

I hold out my arm for her to hold after draping her shawl around her shoulders to leave. It's chilly and I don't want her to catch a cold.

"I'll take you here any time you want." I bend down and place a gentle kiss on her lips before guiding her into the car.

Chapter 26

R *osie*

Once we're in the car, I can't hold myself back anymore. It's been physically painful, going two full days since our kiss and not being able to do it again.

I don't bother with a seatbelt, climbing onto Finnegan's lap as soon as we're on the road.

"This car better not be taking me home." I say, an edge of command in my voice as I fist my hands in my orc's hair.

He quickly presses the buzzer to speak to the driver, telling him to take us straight to the final destination.

"That's a good boy," I whisper in his ear before trailing kisses down his neck.

"Oh, fuck." He grips my hips, tightly pulling me against him. Our lips meet in a desperate clash, eager tongues tangling.

Finnegan pulls back after a few minutes when a red light flashes above the door.

"I'm so fucking sorry but I live really close to the restaurant."

I burst out in laughter, looking down at myself and my hiked up dress. Wow, I really laid it on him there. I climb off of him with as much grace as I can manage. I'm worried I've overdone it, but he leans over and kisses me again before he opens the door to the crisp night air.

Taking his hand, I slip out of the car. Finnegan reaches behind me, grabbing my forgotten purse and shawl.

"Whoops," My head is really not with it, but the cold air is sobering me up. As is the behemoth of a house in front of me.

"This is your house?!"

It's completely detached, with space all around. A glance tells me that we're up on a hill of some sort. It's sleek and modern, a study in architecture and filled with giant window panels in place of walls.

"Come inside, it's cold." He wraps my shawl around me, rubbing my arms and guiding me into the front door.

Finnegan guides me past the grand foyer and staircase and into a huge open living space.

I was correct about the hill. This side of the home showcases a stunning view of the city below, a mass of twinkling lights. There are different shapes flying in the sky sporadically, shadows in the night.

"What kind of birds are those?" I ask, walking up close to the window to get a better look.

Something I've said is amusing to Finnegan. He loses it, bending over at the hip with laughter.

"I don't get what's so funny..."

"Sorry, sweetie." He comes over to me and strokes my hair softly. I like the pet name, it's cute and it gives me butterflies in my stomach. "It's just, when I tell you what they are you'll get it. But, sweetie, think about all the different types of monsters that you've met. How many of them have wings?"

"*Oh.*"

"Yeah."

I also burst out in laughter at my stupidity. Whilst my best friend is mated to a monster, I sometimes forget that

that doesn't mean I know every little thing about this side of the city.

Finnegan holds me from behind once our laughter dies down, and we watch the city for a minute.

"I'm gonna go get us some water so that we're not dying in the morning." He kisses my cheek. "Then we need to have a chat, there's something I need to talk to you about."

He's gone in a blur, and I wander around while I wait.

I'm not too nervous, I'm sure I know what the talk is about. In fact, I should have been the one to bring it up, I've been taking the lead more than he has in that department.

He pops back into the room, two water glasses in hand, and gestures to the couch behind him for us to sit.

I gulp down some of the water before sitting next to him. We probably shouldn't be talking about this when we've had so much wine. But there's no going back now, and I'm not leaving here without having some fun with my orc.

"There's something that I need to tell you." He says, stroking my knee where it rests against his legs.

"OK." I'll let him say what he needs to, he's probably been rehearsing it anyway.

"I am sorry for keeping this from you, but I thought it might scare you off and I wanted you to like me for me before it got in the way." Oh, wow. I wonder what sort of kink he's hiding. I sit forward in my seat, stroking his hair reassuringly. "I noticed it the first day that we met. I smelled your scent and I knew."

Wait, what?

"We're mates, Rosie."

I think I stop breathing. My hand slackens in his hair, but I don't pull away.

We're mates? *Mates*?

"Like... Flora and...?" My voice trails off, unsure if I should even finish that sentence.

"I know it's a shock. I hope you can understand why I kept it from you initially."

He might continue talking but I'm not hearing him anymore.

It all makes sense now. The way he followed me, came to my café, tried to help me out with the investment.

I search inside myself, but I'm not unhappy about it. It's just... it's a shock.

I'm not sure if I'm supposed to say something. The last thing I want is to hurt his feelings after him being so vulnerable with me. And to think, I thought that we were about to have a kink talk before getting into bed together.

Catching back up with myself in the moment, I start to stroke Finnegan's hair again to reassure him.

"Sorry," I say. "It's just a lot to process."

"I understand." He tentatively runs his hand up and down my leg in soothing strokes. "I can take you home if you need time to process. Or I could put you up in a guest bedroom here."

"I don't want to go home, Fin." I scooch a little closer so that we're pressed flush against one another. "I'm not sad about this, just in shock. But a guest room sounds perfect for tonight. Tomorrow is Saturday, neither of us are working. Let's spend that time together and see how we're doing then?"

Chapter 27

Finnegan

Leaning against the door frame to one of my guest rooms, I say goodnight to Rosie, showing her where everything is and giving her an old t-shirt to sleep in.

"Well, I'm just down the hall if you need anything." I say, moving to shut the door.

"Wait!" She runs around the bed, pulling me down in a kiss. It's bittersweet, and I pour all of my affection for her into it. "It's just that I need some space alone to think, OK? This isn't a rejection."

I nod, pulling the door shut with a click.

Hearing her words and believing them are two different things. But I am fully aware that she hasn't had the same privilege of the weeks to process this that I have. It's completely valid for her to ask for some time to form her own thoughts. Especially for a human, this is so foreign to what she knows.

That doesn't mean that I'm not feeling a bit down about it. When I get in my room I switch on some music. There's a new artist at the label that I've been meaning to listen to, and we need to make a decision on how much funding to allot to his next record.

Once I'm washed and changed into some pajama pants, I get into bed with my digital drawing pad and sketch for a bit, to take my mind off things. My eyes start to droop pretty quickly, and I just shut them for a minute.

Tiptoeing footsteps down the hallway wake me up, the creak of my door following them. I startle, realizing that I fell asleep while drawing. The light from the hallway glows against Rosie's back as she enters the room.

"Can I sleep with you?" She asks, toying with the bottom of my shirt she's wearing. "Just to snuggle."

I place my drawing pad and pen on the nightstand and scoot back, pulling the sheet up and gesturing for her to get in.

Rosie climbs in, cuddling up to my chest and resting her head there. I easily fall back to sleep, my mate wrapped in my arms and surrounded by her scent.

Chapter 28

Rosie

Waking up wrapped in my mate's arms feels significant. There was a special sort of peace that washed over me when I cuddled up to him last night. It's definitely something that I could get used to.

I had lasted a couple of hours in the guest room, tossing and turning, ruminating the new information. The more I lay there, the more ridiculous I felt.

The male that I was falling for had just confessed to me that we were biologically predetermined to be together, and I just walked away? Asked for some space? The shock had clearly gone to my head.

Once I realized I was being a complete idiot, I knew I couldn't just stay in the bed alone, knowing that he was probably freaking out in the other room.

Finnegan is so cozy and soft beneath me. I don't think I realized that he was topless last night. The blanket is down around his waist now, and I can properly see his chest. His nipples are a darker shade of green than his skin, both pierced through with metal bars. It's a wonder that my hair didn't get caught in those last night.

A smattering of black hair grows across his chest and down his chiseled abs. He's certainly ripped for a male who works a desk job. Finnegan is soft to the touch though, muscled in a way that shows he is strong, but also not obsessively at the gym.

I'm incredibly attracted to this giant orc in bed next to me, and it's not that I don't want to fuck him. But I do think there is a lot that we still need to talk about before we take that next step. Before, he was just a guy that I wanted to fuck and maybe date for a while. Knowing that we're mates changes things, and I need to be sure that we communicate and do right by one another.

I feel a little guilty about last night though, so I decide to make him breakfast to show that I do care. Slipping out of the sheets, I manage not to disturb him. He snores gently as I creep out of the room and back down to the kitchen to see what I'm working with.

Luckily, his fridge is well stocked. I search around some cupboards until I find everything I need. He has a pretty great kitchen setup for someone who hasn't claimed to be a great cook.

I set the griddle on to heat while I whisk up some eggs. We always give him a sneakily bigger portion than normal at the café, but I wonder if even that is enough for him. So I put on some extra slices of bacon and crack a few more eggs into the bowl.

Using the moment of peace while the bacon gets crispy and it's too soon to put the eggs on, I brew a pot of coffee. I'm just stirring in the milk to a cup when I hear Finnegan coming down the stairs, a slouched over hulking male.

"I thought the water would help," he says, rubbing at his head.

"Here." I pass him the cup of coffee that I had just made for myself. "You look like you need it."

He takes the cup in one hand, pulling me against him with the other as he kisses me on the top of the head.

"It smells really good."

"It won't smell good for long if you don't let me go." I tease, smacking him on the ass.

"I'll just watch. Pretend I'm not here." Finnegan walks around the island and sits on a bar stool while I get back to work.

"Oh wow." He says after his first bite. I've served us at the bar so that it's easy to clean up after. "I had the stuff in there to make this taste so good?"

"It's nothing special." I laugh, brushing his hair out of his face.

I've learned two things about my mate this morning. One, he is not functioning until he has his coffee. Two, he is very easily impressed in the kitchen.

"This bacon, though." He takes another bite, his eyes rolling back in his head as he moans.

How am I supposed to not bang him on the spot when he is behaving like this.

"Thanks, it's coated in honey and some spices."

"Hmm," he continues enjoying his food. It takes us the same amount of time to finish two very different sized portions.

"Let me clean up and make us some more coffee." Finnegan kisses me on the head again. "Go get cozy on the couch."

I won't complain about that. Settling myself onto the cushions, I pull the throw blanket onto my lap and get comfy. The problem with these monster houses is that their couches are far too comfortable. The back of the seat goes above my head, so it's too easy to snuggle in against the cushion.

Finnegan comes back after a bit, waking me gently from a snooze to pull me onto his lap. I curl up there drifting in and out of sleep as the TV plays in the background. I can hear him sipping on a coffee, but it's a comforting sound. Once he settles the mug down, he starts to play with my hair, smoothing out any tangles and rubbing my scalp.

I can't help my answering groan, shifting so that he can get a better angle.

"What would it be like?" I ask. "Our lives together? Would it be like this?"

"On the weekends, maybe." He replies, continuing with his attentions on my hair. "But I won't lie, I do work a lot. Although, I think that's the same for you too."

"Hmm..." I don't agree or disagree aloud, but we both know that's right.

"It's not up to me alone, though, what our life would look like. There's a couple things in my control though that I can tell you. We'd be set financially. Anything you want to do, any dreams that you have, I would one hundred percent support you with. I'd be caring and attentive, and I'd always try to communicate with you if there is something I'm not happy with."

I sit up, needing to look at him for this conversation. Searching his dark green eyes, I see nothing but genuine care there.

"Well, you're right that I do work a lot. And I don't know about you, but that gets pretty lonely for me. I work with so many people that when I enter my own space in the evenings it feels too empty. It would be nice to have someone to come home to, to spend lazy Saturday mornings like this with."

I wrap my arms around his neck, sitting up on my knees so that we are at eye level. The late morning sunlight washes over the room, his eyes glowing as they gaze back at me. His tusks gleaming and shifting as he smiles. He's beautiful, my mate.

"That's all I want, Rosie." He tugs me so that I am pressed flush against him. "I want you in my life, to be here after work and on the weekends. We can go out to eat on a Saturday night and sleep in on a Sunday morning. You don't even have to cook, we can order in breakfast and laze about, completely shut off from the world."

I tuck my head into the hollow of his neck and breathe him in.

"There's only one other thing I want to clarify then, before we give this a proper try."

The hope in his eyes as I say it makes my heart want to burst.

"Anything."

"Last night when you sat me down to talk, I was expecting a very different conversation." His brow furrows, and I need to spell it out for him. "Do you have any preferences, in the bedroom?" I pointedly glance down at his crotch.

Chapter 29

F*innegan*

"Oh," I wasn't expecting that. But I am always happy to have that conversation. "I'm a switch, so I'm happy with whatever you are, sweetie."

"We both know that's not how that works." She chuckles. "Come now, you told me that you were going to give me open communication."

"You're right." I sigh, running a hand over my face. "You're not going to scare me off."

"OK," I take a deep breath, figuring out how best to phrase what I like. "I like there to always be a Dom/sub dynamic, no matter which part I'm playing, and I don't mind it switching back and forth throughout a scene."

"That's good," she continues to stroke my hair except it's feeling a lot more like praise now. "I'm pretty much the same when it comes to dynamics. What about specific kinks?"

"I like to be praised. I was really into you calling me a good boy in the car last night." I relax the tension in my body, content to rest and open up to her now. "If I'm being dominant, I want to be rough and primal about it. And I have a little bit of an exhibitionist streak. But if I'm being honest, I haven't ever found a partner to explore my submissiveness with before."

"I'm the same." She laughs, a twinkling sound. "I've plenty of experience playing the dominant role, and I would love to explore that more with you. But I'm kind of a brat when it comes to being submissive myself."

"What kind of ideas do you have in mind?"

"I'm more of a pleasure Domme, Finnegan." Oh fuck, she was going to kill me and I would be grateful for it. This is the exact sort of fantasy that I've played in my mind. "Edging you, for a start. I would love to take my time with it, spend hours bringing you to the point of coming. How does that sound?"

Rosie bites on her lip as she waits for me to answer. I pull her against me in a hot, searing kiss. Flipping us so that she is pressed beneath me on the couch, my body caging her in.

"Nuh uh, big boy." She points her finger against my chest. "Up. I want your clothes off and you on your knees before me."

I do as I am told, stripping off and perching on the ground before her.

"Good boy." She praises me, patting me on the head and stroking me there. "Now, let's see what we are working with."

Rosie pointedly looks to my crotch, and I cross my arms behind my back so as not to block her view. I wonder what she thinks of my cock. I can imagine that it's very different to a human man's.

It's green like the rest of me, although if she pulls my foreskin back she will see that it's black underneath. My whole shaft is covered in hard little nubs, but the layer of skin on top makes them more pleasurable than anything else. And then there's my knot, the large ring around the base that will expand when I cum, locking us together.

"This will do." Rosie grips my cock in her hands, slowly stroking. My knees almost buckle at the first touch, the stroking already hardening me to a painful point. I'm at the perfect height for her, kneeling like this, she doesn't even need to bend.

"We're going to use the traffic light system. If you need me to slow down or stop."

"OK. I know that." My abs tighten as she stops her movement, looking at me expectantly. "Orange to slow, red to stop."

"Good boy."

A shiver runs down my spine at her words.

"Sit up on the couch and get comfortable. We'll take this first try nice and easy, OK?"

I settle down onto the couch, wiggling until I'm comfortable, just like she said.

Rosie palms my cock, stroking me with varying intensities until I am a writhing mess beneath her.

"Fuck, Rosie." I pant, gripping her ass beneath my t-shirt. "I'm going to—ahh!"

I shout as she drops my cock, pulling away from me and looking at me through hooded lids. Her cheeks are flushed, and I can see how much it has affected her. My balls throb and tighten, my cock twitching. All I want to do is grip my cock in hand and finish myself off.

But the warning look in Rosie's eyes tells me all I need to know. This isn't about me cumming. Not yet, anyway.

"Eyes on me." I tear my gaze from my twitching cock and look at my mate. Something primal in me, some alpha instinct preens at seeing her in my clothes, my t-shirt reaching below her knees like a dress. She bunches up the fabric at her hips, letting a little more leg peek out, before sliding it over her head.

My mate stands in front of me in nothing but her panties and she is pure sin. She smirks, showing me another facet of her personality to tuck away. Her breasts hang heavy and I can't bear sitting here while she stands before me like that. I want to sink my fingers into her plush body and hold her close.

"Hands behind your back." She commands, her eyes flicking to my twitching fingers. "You're going to be a good boy and keep those back there. Aren't you?"

"Yes."

She hooks her fingers through the lace waistband of her panties, and I know I'm a goner. They hit the floor beneath her, and I can see how damp they've become. Is that just from stroking my cock?

Rosie makes her way back to me, straddling my lap as she takes my cock in her hands again. She alternates between that and rubbing her slick pussy against it. Every time I am close to cumming, she slows down or pulls back.

It feels like hours have passed before she finally keeps going, pushing me past the point where she normally stops. There are tears streaming down my face, but I still keep my hands behind my back. My cock is slick from her wetness, and the easy glide of her hands sends me into the most desperate orgasm of my life.

Chapter 30

R *osie*

Finnegan is beautiful beneath me, completely undone and covered in sweat and cum.

"Good boy," I soothe him gently stroking and petting him until his breathing becomes a little less erratic. "Wait here."

I head to the kitchen to get some paper towels and a glass of water, washing my hands while I'm there too.

Checking the time, I'm surprised that it's well past lunch and encroaching into dinner territory.

When I come back, I find him drifting in and out of consciousness. I wipe him down with the paper towels, it's efficient enough and I don't know where the wash cloths are yet.

"You did so well," I tell him. "You lasted so long for me."

His eyes flicker open at that, his poor hands still tucked behind his back. I guide them out, rubbing and massaging them to make sure his circulation is alright. I pass him the water, keeping my hands close in case he drops the glass while he drinks.

"Fuck, Rosie. That was..." his voice sounds strained. Which makes sense after all the whimpering and moaning he did for me.

"I'm going to order us dinner." I tell him. "You just curl up here for a little bit and rest, OK?"

He nods sleepily as I take his water glass and guide him to lay down on the couch properly. I pull the throw blanket from earlier over him and stroke his hair back off his face. I'm still floored with how well he submitted for me, this huge male.

I'm exhausted from edging him, too. It made me so horny, but I wanted to focus on him and see how he responded. It was his first time doing anything like that, and I am so grateful for his trust.

Tossing my t-shirt back on, I grab my phone from the kitchen and realize that I can't place an order. There's no way that my human delivery app is going to work on the monster side of the city.

If I'm being honest, Finnegan doesn't look like he's up for eating yet anyway. I curl up next to him on the couch, practically lying on top of him and taking a little nap.

"Rosie? Sweetie, we should probably wake up." I feel like a ton of bricks have crushed my head as I try to open my eyes. The sky is dark outside and I realize that we must have slept for hours. Shit, I should have set an alarm.

Finnegan's hand is buried up my t-shirt, stroking my back in long swoops that are very much not conducive to waking up.

"That feels good." I say, snuggling into his chest even more.

His stomach grumbles beneath me.

"Sorry, I went to order food but I couldn't 'cause my app didn't work here. So I took a nap instead."

Finnegan chuckles, sounding much more refreshed than I feel. He stretches, shifting us, but in his hand is a phone when he relaxes again. So I guess it's worth it.

"Pizza?" I ask with a sweet tone, hoping he'll buy into it.

"You got it, sweetie." He kisses my head and places the order.

We lounge on the couch until the doorbell rings. I get up to answer, but Finnegan insists on getting it. He tosses his pajama pants back on and pads to the door, coming back with three pizza boxes in hand. Normally, I would say that is overkill, but he does seem to have a voracious appetite.

Our meal is gone quickly. We eat on the couch and watch some reality TV. It's fun to watch the different shows that they have here, to learn about all the different monster characters.

I couldn't be happier with how the sex went earlier. It's a big thing for me, and I really didn't want to be tied down to someone who I wasn't compatible with in that way. But so far, it seems like we really do match each other.

"How are you feeling?" I ask him after a couple more episodes.

"Good. Refreshed."

I move onto my knees, sitting up so that we're at eye level when we speak.

"Was there anything that you didn't like? Or even something that you thought you would like more but wouldn't want to try again?"

He shakes his head, "Not unless you count that I'm annoyed you didn't get to cum."

"It wasn't about me." I argue.

"Hmm…" He shrugs, as if to say we can agree to disagree on that one. "Let's go to bed."

Finnegan sets me up in his bathroom with everything I might need, before going to use a guest one. It's sweet that he makes sure I have what I need.

I'm just finishing up when he creeps back into the room behind me, his green form showing in the mirror. He bends over me, kissing my neck and gripping my waist to pull me back against him. My pussy comes to life at his touch, wetness pooling there quickly as he palms my breasts through my t-shirt. It's odd to see how he towers over me, how different we are on the outside.

Turning in his arms, I look up at my orc mate. His leathery soft skin is smooth under my fingers as I run them up his waist.

"I want to try this." I say, holding him firmly and leaning back to look at him properly. "Dating you, at least at first. Spend the next week or so just dating, to get a feel of how we slot together."

Finnegan's smile is incandescent, his tusks poking high as it widens even further.

"Oh, Rosie." He picks me up, swinging me over his shoulder with a laugh. "I'm going to treat you so right. I'll make sure that you are so happy with me."

I squeal as he throws me onto the bed, crawling over me and caging me in with his massive body. I barely have a second to think before Finnegan shoves my shirt over my hips and brings his head between my thighs, my laughter shifting to moans.

"Oh, Fin!" My hands grip his hair tightly as he licks and sucks, bringing the most intense pleasure to my core. The hours of neglect that I gave my pussy earlier today means that my orgasm is quick to build.

Finnegan pushes one of his long, thick fingers into my pussy, curling it upward and pressing firmly. It only brings more intensity to his attention on my clit. I cry out as my orgasm rips through me, shocked at how quickly it built.

"S-stop," I have to tell him as he continues to lick my oversensitive clit. "I need, a... second."

He looks up at me, lifting his head with a self-satisfied grin. "I've been dying to taste you."

Barely managing a nod, I pull his face to mine and kiss him deeply. My body still sings in a chorus of tingles, but the solid weight of my mate keeps me grounded. After a moment, Finnegan starts to move his finger in my pussy, adding another to the mix as he fucks me through our kiss.

Grinding against his hand, I lose myself to the sensations. I grip his hair tightly and nibble on his lips and jaw as I moan and writhe against him. I'm beyond words now as I cum again, melting into a puddle beneath him.

His hard cock bumps against me through his pajama pants. I reach down, shoving his pants over his hips and gripping his textured shaft.

"Clothes," he gasps. "Off."

My t-shirt is off and on the floor next to his quickly discarded pajama pants in a matter of seconds. I didn't get to truly appreciate his full form earlier, but as he stands over me now I can't help but do that. Thick thighs frame his massive, ridged cock, which I'm not even sure that I will be able to take. Chiseled abs meet huge pecs with his pierced nipples, then his enormous biceps and thick forearms. My mate is huge, muscled in a way that shows strength and soft when he is relaxed. I should find him a terrifying monster, but he is anything but.

"I am..." I start to say. "You are so fucking hot, Fin."

My gaze is drawn back to his face as he grins, white fangs showing from inside his mouth. Even those don't scare me. I feel so safe with him, a natural trust having formed over these past few weeks.

Finnegan settles into the bed sitting up, resting his back against the headboard. He easily picks me up along the way and settles me on his lap. His cock presses against my stomach, dragging a long line as he raises me up to kiss him.

Tilting my hips a little, I manage to grind up against him, but I'm too wet for there to be enough friction.

"I wanted to play with these so bad earlier." He arches my back and sucks on my nipple, leaving a little bite in his wake before moving onto the other.

"Fin, please." I beg, gripping his shoulders tightly.

"What do you need, petal?" He's teasing me, but I almost cry in my desperation.

"You." I whimper as he bites down on my nipple again. "I need you. Please, fuck me."

His kisses trail up my chest and to my neck as he lowers me back down slowly. He shifts, and his cock is pressing against my pussy. I try to shift, to sink down onto him, but he holds me still. My hips won't move unless he allows it.

"Eyes on me." The sliver of command in his voice tells me to obey. Finnegan is sweet in submission, but when he takes control, I am putty. His to command.

His dark green orbs are almost entirely black, his pupils blown out as he looks at me. Finally, he lowers me slowly onto his cock. My eyes flutter shut with the blissful stretch. He immediately stops and I realize my mistake. I open them up and do my best to keep them that way and he stretches me out.

My hands cling to his neck as he starts to move me up and down his shaft, his grip on my ass cheeks tight and spreading me wide for him. It's intense, staring into his eyes as we fuck for the first time. I lose myself in the sensations, his eyes the only thing grounding me.

The ridges on his cock stroke and massage me from the inside, and it sets all of my nerves alight. It's not long before he is bucking up into me, his thrusts becoming sporadic.

"I—ah," He hisses with another bump, and I take him deeper. Fuck, there's more of him? I stretch a little to watch where he enters me, I still haven't taken the big ring at the base. I already feel so stretched full, but I want all of him. He finally manages to finish his sentence, "do you—will you take my knot?"

"Yes, please." I assume that he's talking about the same thing as me. And I'm right, he eases me, ever so slowly over his knot. It's not painful like I might have suspected, but the pressure is intense. He rocks up into me, relaxing his grip now that we are flush together. His knot presses against my sensitive walls, and I reach down to rub my clit as we move together.

I stroke myself faster, seeing that Finnegan is close to the edge. He bucks against me, gripping my hips in place and holding me tight against him as we cum together. A weird sort of pressure builds and builds around my opening, a vacuum sealing me tight with his cock still inside me.

I nearly scream with the intensity, the pressure on my clit making another orgasm wash over me quickly. Finnegan's cock is still spurting warm cum inside me, the heat almost burning as I feel it continue.

"W—what..?" I panic, feeling trapped and struggling to find my words.

"Shh, it's OK." He strokes my back and tries to settle me on his chest.

"No," I push back. "What's happening?"

I can tell that Finnegan is pushing through his own pleasure, his cum still spurting inside me as I wriggle.

"I knotted you, petal." He brushes my sweat damp hair out of my face. "You said yes. I'm sorry I can't stop it now. W—we... ahh, oh," he bucks against me again and I see stars as another orgasm forces its way through me. "We need to stay s—still if you need it to s—"

We both cry out again as a slight shift causes another torrent of pleasure.

My panic eases, my instincts taking over now that I know that there isn't something wrong. I lean back, testing how much I can grind without setting us off, enjoying the pressure and pleasure. Circling my hips does the trick.

I place my hands on his chest and move my hips in a crescent moon shape, leaning back so that the pressure isn't too much on my clit. It's fucking amazing. I accidentally make us cum a few more times until I collapse against his chest, snuggling in and waiting it out like he suggested.

If the sex is going to be like this every time, I am going to become an addict.

Chapter 31

The designer walks around the space with Rosie. She's a nymph with an eye for design that we've used on other projects before, but if Rosie isn't happy we can go with someone else.

I felt a little bad, making a call to her on a Sunday morning and expecting her to meet us in the human side of the city. But if we didn't do this today, it would be a week until we had the opportunity again, with Rosie's café closing only on Sundays.

We chatted about that in the car ride over here, actually. How making some more hires was going to be needed with her taking a step back from the running of this location, and how she might as well open on Sundays too in that case.

It was strange, parking my car around the back and using the private entrance. When we woke up this morning, still tangled in one another, I had felt so refreshed. And so grateful to have such a willing and accepting mate. Once I drank my coffee, I had explained that I thought we could get the designer in today so that she had the week to work on the plans for the new location.

Rosie had worn her dress from dinner on Friday night and taken a shower and changed when we got to her place. We were going to need to get her some things to keep at mine. Especially because I want nothing more than to have her there every night. But I also need to respect her boundaries. This is new for both of us, we've both been single for a long time, and it would be good to ease into things slowly. Or well, more slowly than my alpha instincts are screaming at me to do.

"Let me make you dinner." She says now, after seeing the designer out of the front door and locking up.

"Well I'm hardly going to say no to that."

Rosie puts together a lasagna, popping it in the oven and coming to join me on the couch. We kiss, and play, nothing too intense. But it is so comfortable and easy.

After a delicious meal and an hour of chatting, I head back home to my own house. Leaving Rosie with a lingering goodbye kiss.

I can't believe how lucky I am, that she has accepted me so much already.

It feels a little lonely, switching on the lights to my empty house, but the comforting and decadent scent of my mate permeates the air.

Chapter 32

R*osie*

The café is busy today, and I almost miss the delivery guy trying to squeeze in the door with an enormous bouquet of flowers. I get Ben to cover the register and quickly rush to the man with the flowers.

"Sorry, I almost didn't see you!" I swing my towel over my shoulder and peek around the flowers to see his face. "Do you need help finding an address? I know the area pretty well."

"This is Rosie's café, right?" He says, looking around the space. "Just looking for Rosie and then I'll be on my way."

"Oh!" I blink, they're for me? I hold up my name tag. "That's me."

"Great." He passes a pad for me to sign and passes the heavy bouquet to me. Leaving the shop without a word.

"Thank you!" I call after him.

We are overrun with customers, but I need to get these upstairs without anyone seeing.

The gorgeous blooms fit in well with my apartment, I realize as I set them down on the coffee table. They smell beautiful, a mix of roses dotted in with many other colorful stems. There's a card tucked into the ribbon on the side, and I excitedly snatch it up.

I hope you like gifts, because I want to spoil you.
Yours, Fin

I quickly text him a picture and a thank you message. They're beautiful, and I want to sit up here with them for the rest of the day.

There are interviews this afternoon, though. I put out a job ad last night and already I have a few people to potentially hire for the café.

The flowers were a lovely surprise yesterday, especially since neither of us had time to hang out after work.

But when another package arrives today, I wonder if I need to get a bigger apartment for all this. He did warn me in his card though.

It's a rectangular shaped box with a ribbon tied around it. I rush up to my apartment right away to open it.

I'm shocked to see gorgeous navy silk when I open the box. A card is on top with an invite to a charity gala this evening, a slip of paper attached with a note from Finnegan asking me to join him.

Tossing the card aside, I pull out the fabric. It's a beautiful silk gown, far nicer than anything I own, and I'm so grateful that he thought to give me an outfit, because I would have been panicking about what to wear.

There is a set of matching heels and what appears to be a jewelry box. Oh, shit.

I set it down on the counter and carefully open the lid. It's breathtaking. A stunning silver necklace with a spattering of bright blue jewels, and matching earrings pinned above.

There are two certificates of authenticity at the bottom of the box, outlining that they are platinum and sapphire.

Shit, these are really nice. Am I supposed to not accept them? What's appropriate here? We've only been on one date.

That's not how it works for him though, is it? We're mates, and while I'm coming to terms with everything, he sees me as a life partner already.

No pressure.

I call Flora, catching her up on the past four days in the briefest way possible. She insists on coming over to help me get ready.

Chapter 33

I have the car pull up out the back of Rosie's place to pick her up again, the street still busy outside in the early evening.

One thing is for certain, I am going to be the one to open her door for her tonight. I tell the driver as much as I hop out to wait for her.

My jaw nearly hits the floor when she steps outside to meet me. The dress I picked for her hugs her curves, the navy silk a shimmering pool on the ground. She wears her hair pinned down her back in loose waves, the jewelry I bought her on full display.

"You look... incredible." I hold out my hands to her and give her a gentle kiss, careful not to disturb her makeup. I hold her in place as I continue to look at her. "The jewelry matches your eyes perfectly."

"It's beautiful," she rests her hand on her throat atop the jewels. "Thank you so much."

I hold open the car door for her, getting settled in the back seat together.

"Thank *you*," I say with emphasis. "For coming at such short notice."

Pulling out my tablet from the side drawer, I open my email and scroll through to find the files.

"I have something to show you. The designer has been in the space the past couple days, and she has some plans."

"Ooh," Rosie nearly snatches it out of my hand to look.

We spend the car ride going through notes on the plans, Rosie deciding to only make a couple smaller changes. But we are able to finalize things and send them back to the designer by the time we get to the event.

It's an event that I have historically never taken a date to. If I'm being honest, I don't take dates to anything, really. So when we get to the ballroom for the gala, we get quite a lot of stares. Not just because Rosie is a human, but because most people are shocked to see me with *anyone*.

She is a little hesitant at first, but we get some drinks and find a group of my colleagues to mingle with before the meal. Once she has assessed that she is perfectly safe, Rosie really shines.

It's not that she hasn't told me that she is good with people, I mean I've seen her warm many a soul in her café. But seeing her networking at an event like this is a sight to behold. She's charming, and a group of people quickly form, hanging on her every word.

When we are told to take our seats for the meal, a wash of disappointment waves over them. And when one of the females, a bright haired witch, realizes that she is sitting next to Rosie, she's excited. I barely get a look in, sitting back and letting her have her fun, a steady presence at her back.

I'm not bad with people, per se, I certainly wouldn't have my job if I was. But I was nowhere near the scale that she works at. It's great to see her in her element, and I am again confident in my decision to invest in her café. If she isn't held back by working in the space herself then she is free to network on this sort of level.

The meal flows quickly, the auction portion the same. We bid on a trip to a beach destination, a private villa over the water. It gets priced quite high, but I can tell that Rosie is having fun so I give her the paddle and tell her that the sky is the limit. It's for charity, anyway.

When we get into the car at the end of the night, Rosie asks to come back to mine, as if it's even a question.

Chapter 34

R *osie*

We're not quite as desperate in the car ride to Finnegan's house tonight. But we do still make out quite heavily in the back seat.

I sit sideways on his lap, my dress too long for anything else. It was so hard to keep my hands off him in this tux. My fingers slip over the silk lapel, the perfect matching shade to my dress.

"You really are good with people." He voices, once I allow him a moment to breathe.

"Hmm..." I agree, pulling him back in for more kissing. I truly cannot get enough of him. I'm excited for him to knot me again tonight too. It was initially a shock, and yes I panicked a little, but it was so good once I understood what was happening.

He had apologized afterward, for assuming that I knew what would happen. But it was honestly fine.

Finnegan breaks our kiss, moving down my neck instead and breathing me in.

"What do I smell like?" I ask, getting comfy in the position, content to let him breathe me in if he wanted. "You said I had a scent, that's how you knew we were mates."

He takes a long inhale, waiting a few moments before answering.

"You smell rich, it's complex. A berry red wine with a hint of spices. And when you're turned on..." He trails a hand up my leg, moving to whisper in my ear. "It sweetens, develops into something much more fruity."

His whisper sends a shiver down my spine, and it takes me a second to realize what he's said.

"You can smell when I'm *horny*?!"

At his answering nod, I blush a furious red. All of the times that I thought I was being coy, at the café... no, even at that party! He could smell it, the whole time, how fucking turned on I was for him.

"It's OK," he laughs at my expense. Asshole. "It was good for my ego when you were ignoring me."

"Ugh," I bury my head in his chest, hiding from him. At least I know now that he is scenting me, and I don't mind if he knows I'm turned on anymore.

The car pulls to a stop at that moment, the red light turning on to signal we've arrived at the house. It's only my second time visiting, but I feel comfortable enough now, hopping out of the car and walking to the door on my own. I even have my purse.

Finnegan follows quickly, his tablet and some work things in hand. He must have gotten ready at the studio before heading out. I'm a little cold, having forgotten to grab a shawl on my way out earlier but we're quickly inside and into the warmth of the house.

"Want another glass of wine?"

I nod, heading up the stairs to get dressed in something more comfortable. "Be back in a sec."

Finnegan's room is more clean, modern lines. His closet almost clinical with how tidy and clean it is. I'd teased him about being a clean freak but he admitted to having a maid who comes while he's at work. They certainly earn their pay check, that's for sure.

Slipping out of my dress, I hang it up and lay my jewelry out on a shelf. I run my fingers over the beautiful jewels again, touched that he thought to match my eyes. I pull down a soft button up from his more casual shirt selection and slip on the light blue cotton, leaving it a little unbuttoned and rolling up the sleeves. Not bothering to take off my makeup yet, I head back downstairs.

"Fuck, you look hot." Finnegan eyes me up as I join him in the room again. He's taken off his jacket, rolling up his own sleeves too. His corded forearms look far too sexy as he holds out a glass of wine to me.

We sit on the couch that faces the view outside, watching the flying Monsters in the sky, the stars high above them. I tuck my knees beneath me as we chat, content to debrief on our evening. We gossip about the different people at the gala, and Finnegan catches me up on how he knows some of them, or some drama he's heard about them.

"You're quite the gossip, aren't you?" I tease.

"I do think that there are two pretty big gossips in this room."

I pretend to look shocked, but we both know that it's true. Everything aside with us being mates and all, it's really nice to have a friend again. Flora hasn't had as much time for me since meeting Sebastian, and I don't begrudge her that at all, but it's been pretty lonely.

Having someone to go to things with, to get home and gossip with afterwards... it's really nice. My chest warms as I look at my orc, kneeling up and kissing him softly.

"I've had fun tonight," I say. Stroking his hair back from his face, I'm again struck with how attractive he is. Not in a conventional human sort of way, that's for sure. But his strong cheekbones and jawline, his bushy brows, his gleaming tusks. It all frames the most beautiful deep green eyes that light up when he smirks at me.

It's only been a few weeks since I met him, but I think I'm falling in love with Finnegan.

"You seemed excited about that trip." He pulls me onto his lap so that I'm straddling him, his hands on my hips.

"Yeah! Thank you, it will be so much fun! We'll have to figure out when to book it for." I kiss the corner of his mouth, my lips brushing against his tusk.

"Well, I was thinking that we could go now. Tomorrow, I mean. It would be a good opportunity to test Farrow out with running the café on her own. And by the time we come back, the new café will be nearly complete."

"That soon?" I nibble on my lip with hesitation. "Are you sure you're able to get away from work?"

"Yeah, I might have to do a couple calls while we're gone. But nothing crazy. It doesn't even have to be the trip we won. Honestly, I was probably just going to book us a better version of that and give the value of it to the charity anyway."

His hands stroke my hips soothingly while I think on it. Farrow could do with the experience, and I would be a phone call away if she needed anything.

A little over a year ago, I gave my friend the push she needed with her partner, and look how well that went for her. Maybe it was time to give myself that push.

"OK." I wrap my hands around his neck. "Yeah, let's do it! What do we need to do? Should I look at flights?"

I reach behind myself to grab my phone off the coffee table, but Finnegan snags it mid air and settles me back around his neck.

"No, sweetie. You don't do things like book flights anymore." He picks up his own phone, recording a voice note and sending it to his assistant. "Cynthia will sort out all the details, it's why I pay her."

Seeing him take charge like that sends flutters to my core. It sets an idea running in my head.

"I need you." I tug his head down so that I can speak into his ear. "Can you take charge for a little? Be a bit rough with me?"

Finnegan's hands tighten on my waist, fingers digging in. "Safe word?"

"Peanuts." He doesn't chuckle at that or ask any questions. A switch flicking and his demeanor changing.

A large hand wraps around my neck, tugging me up onto my knees to meet him in a bruising kiss. Heat pools in my core, my panties dampening, as his fangs scrape against my lips in a rough caress.

He stands abruptly, throwing me off center as he picks me up with him, one hand still wrapped firmly around my neck. I grip him tightly as he walks us into the dining room, setting me on the table.

Finnegan swings me around, moving me like I'm a doll and settling me so that I'm laying on the table, my head at his hips. He bends forward, smothering my face with his crotch, his hard dick pressing against me and cutting off my breath.

The fabric of the shirt I'm wearing pulls taut before I hear a ripping sound and cold air hits my chest. My chest burns with the lack of air, but he palms my breasts, pinching my nipples hard before letting me breathe again.

I gasp, my chest heaving, a blissful feeling washing over me.

"Touch yourself," his voice is harsher than normal, laced with command. I move my hands to my nipples, "not there. Rub your clit, I want you ready for me."

My hands do as they're told, pleasure scorching through me as I stroke my slippery pussy.

"That's it." A harsh pain flairs across my breast, and I realize belatedly that he's smacked me there. The burn feels good against my sensitive nipple.

I tip my head back to look at him. He palms his cock through his pants as he watches me through hooded lids. Unzipping his pants, he takes his cock in hand and strokes it with a squeeze on the head.

I'm pulled by the shoulders until my head is hanging off the edge of the table. Between that and the attention my clit is getting, I become lightheaded in the best way.

"Tap the table if you need me to stop." That's all the warning I get before Finnegan is shoving the head of his cock in my mouth, forcing my jaw to open wide.

I try my best to switch to breathing through my nose as he uses my mouth.

"Fuck." He groans, smacking at my breast again and making me jump. The movement gives him more access to push further down my throat. I do my best to relax so that he can get deeper, swirling my tongue around his shaft.

He doesn't thrust, keeping his cock still inside me until he pulls out again and I am gasping for air.

The rush of oxygen makes me dizzy in a pleasurable way. My orgasm flowing over me like a wave.

"I need to stop with my clit for a second."

Instead of replying, Finnegan picks me up again. Somehow I end up with my front down on the table and my legs hanging off. My hips are raised, and his cock slides inside me in one hard thrust. I cry out at the invasion, feeling stuffed to the brim, his knot pressing at my entrance.

Finnegan grips my hips tightly as he pounds in and out of me. I try to hold the table for purchase, but my fingers slip along the glossy wood. All I can do is relax into it and let him fuck me however he wants. It's the exact thing I was asking for. My nipples brush against the table, creating friction with every thrust. I cum again pretty quickly with all the sensations going on, not even in control of that anymore.

His knot presses into me right before he comes, and it's even more intense from this position. I lose count of how many times I orgasm while he continues cumming inside me.

Strong arms lift me up, and Finnegan walks us back to the living room. My legs dangle and the extra weight of my body pushes me down further on his cock. Tears stream down my face from the intensity of the pleasure, but when he settles us on the couch it eases off a little.

He whispers soothing words as he strokes my hair. I lay back against his chest until I fall asleep, his cock still inside me.

Chapter 35

Finnegan

Rosie is fast asleep with her head in my lap while I work on some final reports. If I get these done, I shouldn't have much at all left to do for the full trip. Well, apart from checking with the designer on decorating Rosie's café, but we're both excited about that.

The flight attendant drops by to top off my coffee.

"Anything else I can get you?" She whispers, so as not to disturb my mate.

"Maybe a second coffee, please. I think she'll need it in a minute."

The flight attendant nods and comes back promptly with a steamy cup. I pet Rosie's hair as I finish reading the last report, all I have to do is type up my notes and we're good to go.

This morning passed in a blur. We packed up my things before heading to Rosie's so she could pack and prep Farrow for the time we were going to be away. Farrow was surprised to see me come in from the back with Rosie, her brown eyes widening. But she seemed excited to get to try the role of manager for a bit.

Rosie stirs once I get to typing, as I suspected might happen.

"Hi, sweetie."

She sits up, rubbing at her eyes and looking out the window. We were still over the ocean, a blue unending mass.

"Your coffee should be a good temperature." I suggest, her sleepy brain accepting and picking it up right away. I am jealous that she can sleep so easily, and that she's so small that she can rest in my lap. Even flying private like this, I can't sleep unless it's on the actual bed in the back.

Once I've finished with my notes, Rosie is fully awake with an empty coffee cup. She gives me a cheeky smile that I know spells out trouble.

"We still haven't explored that 'streak of exhibitionism' that you mentioned having, you know." She reaches down to my cock, twisting her body to cover it. It hardened almost instantly at her words, but all the way now with her fingernails gently teasing.

"You keep a look out, and tell me if anyone is coming." She kisses me, intense and lingering, before trailing kisses down my neck, her hands working on releasing my cock.

There's only one attendant on this flight, so I just need to keep an eye out for her. Rosie frees my cock finally, her warm hands stroking me. She scoots back a little bit before bending over and laying back down the way she had been napping. Only this time she is licking my cock like a tasty meal.

I bite my lip to stop myself from groaning. The thrill that the attendant could come in on us heightens my arousal. Rosie's scent is sweet and fruity, which only adds to the heady mix.

I'm quick to come, the excitement winning me over. Which is good, because there is less cum in general to clean up. Rosie sucks me dry, swallowing me down, and I'm almost hard again from just remembering the sight of that.

"Good boy." She praises, zipping my cock back into my pants and kissing me so that I can taste myself on her lips.

Chapter 36

Rosie

Cynthia really pulled out all the stops with this villa.

It's pretty secluded, the other villas close enough that you can see that they exist, but far enough away that you wouldn't see any people on the decking. The building is set up on stilts in the water, and the only way on or off is by boat.

The weather is beautiful, not too hot, so you can sit out in the sunshine all day if you wish. Which is exactly what we did for lunch. The villa is serviced, and the staff came by with lunch once we had properly checked in. It was delicious, lots of fresh tropical fruits and salad.

Now that we've been out in the sun for a bit, I decide to go inside and unpack. I love my colorful apartment back home, but this clean beige aesthetic is perfect for a trip. It feels so calming and relaxing.

Finnegan follows me back inside, and I think it might be the perfect time to show him what I've brought with me.

"I have something to show you." I say, opening my suitcase and starting to put my things in the drawers.

"Oh?" He wraps himself around me from behind. "I know what that tone means." He leans down, scenting me to see if it's something sexual.

"It's OK if you don't want to try it. I won't be offended." I turn to face him. "But it is something that I like to do and I thought you would enjoy."

"I'll let you know if I'm not into it." He leans down, pressing a quick kiss to my forehead.

I take a deep breath, pulling out the packing cube that has it inside. Placing it on the bed, I gesture for him to open it. He sucks in a breath once he realizes what's inside, his mouth twitching in what I think might be a smile.

I sit across from him, pulling the dildo and strap out of the bag and setting it on top. "It's brand new. I haven't used it with anyone else."

"I'm kind of intimidated." He says, his green eyes meeting mine.

"That's sort of the whole point." I point out with a dark chuckle.

"He certainly seems to be into it." Finnegan gestures at his crotch, where his cock is pushing hard against the fabric.

"Now or later?" I move over to him, running my hands through his hair and holding his face tenderly.

"If I say later, I might chicken out."

We decide to take a shower first, strip off our plane clothes and get nice and steamy. Finnegan lathers my shampoo and rinses my hair, content to care for me. We take our time, not needing to rush anything. It's the first day of our vacation, we can completely switch off. No one will bother us unless we call for food. It's our own little secluded paradise.

Finnegan kneels on the floor of the shower, moving me to sit on the stone bench. He spreads my legs wide, slotting between them. He presses a flutter of kisses up and down my thighs before finally pressing the tip of his tongue against my clit. He swirls and sucks until I'm a writhing mess, my head tipped back against the cool tile. When I finally cum, Finnegan is there to drink me in, slowly easing back to standing and washing himself as I sit and watch.

I send him into the bedroom to wait for me once we are dried off. Readying myself, I strap the bright blue dildo around my crotch and hips. I test a few different positions, making sure that it's comfortable before I join him. I want this to be as seamless as possible for his first time.

He's laying on the bed with his cock in hand when I finally find him in the room. We spoke about it in the shower, and I'm going to be gentle with him for this first time.

"Oh," he seems… I don't know actually. His eyes are like saucers in his head as he watches me with my dildo hanging heavy between my legs.

"Is that good? Do you like it?" I walk to the suitcase, rooting through for my bottle of lube. I could have had that prepped, but I wanted him to get used to seeing me with it on first.

"Yes." He almost whimpers. "Holy shit, yes."

"Good boy." I finally locate the little bottle. "This is a warming lube, so it shouldn't be too cold after the first second or two."

I climb onto the foot of the bed, and crawl between his legs. Setting the bottle down next to us, I straddle my Orc's waist and kiss him, nice and slowly to relax him. I let him continue stroking his cock at a slow pace, it might also be something comforting for him.

I pause our kissing for a moment to pour some lube on my fingers. Then I lean back in, tonguing his mouth as my hand stretches down and I rub a circle around his hole.

"Lift your leg up for me, honey." I switch my position so I'm further down now. He's too tall for me to be able to kiss him while I do this. "And your other one. Good boy. I think this will be a good position for your first time, but let me know if you need me to change anything, OK?"

"Yes, I think I'm OK like this." I pour some more lube on my fingers and get to work on teasing his ring. With my other hand, I take his cock from him, running my hand up and down the shaft and I pop his head into my mouth, swirling my tongue around it.

I press one finger into his tight hole, but it isn't too tight of a fit. Probably because he is so big. I add a second finger and massage his inner walls. He squirms beneath me, a series of breathy moans escaping him.

"Just relax," I can hear his breathing getting a bit quicker, but he slows down again at my gentle command. "That's it."

I add a third finger and work on stretching him out, using more lube as I need.

"I think you're ready for me." I stroke his cock lovingly. "Are you still good to go?"

"Yes, please fuck me, Rosie."

I don't need to be told twice. Lubing up my dildo, I start to slowly ease it into him. I've never heard him make a noise like he does, halfway between a moan and a gargled shout. My pussy is soaking, watching where the dildo enters his asshole.

I sooth him with gentle, encouraging phrases, pushing in until I bottom out. Easing his legs out of the death grip he has them in, I place them over my shoulders. They're heavier than I expected, but the weight is grounding.

Once he has relaxed against me and I am sure he is used to the girth, I start to thrust, using his legs for purchase. He curses, his hips bucking against me as he takes his cock in hand.

When I pick up a good pace, Finnegan is like putty beneath me. I nearly cum from the image alone. A giant orc splayed out beneath me and falling apart at my touch, my strap-on easing in and out of him.

His cock begins to spurt a white stream of cum on his chest and stomach as he cries out. It's beautiful, seeing him undone like this. His knot flares, and it's fascinating to watch. But with no resistance meeting it, it goes down quickly.

Easing my thrusting, I slowly pull out of my mate, my breath a little heavy from the exertion and my horniness. It's been a long time since I've been able to do that to someone.

"What did you think?" I ask.

"Fuck, Rosie. That was amazing."

Chapter 37

Being on vacation with Rosie is blissful. The past couple days have been spent lazing in the sun, eating delicious food, chatting about anything and everything, and fucking as much as we feel like.

Rosie has fucked me with the strap-on twice now, and it's been so grounding for me sexually. I didn't realize that it was missing for me before. I knew that I was into submission and had yet to explore that, but this was some-thing I hadn't even considered for myself.

My mate is perfect in every single way.

We spent the morning snorkeling, we saw some different colorful fish and a sea turtle. It was fun to play in the shallows with her, splashing and having fun.

Now we are laying out on the decking in the comfy sun beds drying off. Rosie's hair has turned into wild waves from the salt water, and it's so beautiful. Her skin has bronzed, her freckles more prominent on her face now too.

"Come here," I pull her to me. Kissing her deeply, I push my hand into her panties, stroking her clit until she is crying out my name.

Flipping her so that we are spooning, I lift her leg up high and slide my cock home inside of her. We fuck lazily in the sun, grinding against one another until it is too much for me.

My knot pushes inside her and we snuggle, locked to-gether and cumming over and over.

I'm not sure why she hasn't gone into heat yet, but it's something that I've put off speaking with her about.

"Has Flora ever told you about going into heat?" I ask, after we have rinsed off in the outdoor shower, our lunch ordered and on the way.

"Yes, she has. She told me after her and Sebastian mated, and when I told her about you she reminded me again. I'm glad that I'll know what to expect at least." She squeezes her damp hair with a towel. "Why? Do you think I'm showing signs?"

She looks down at herself, as if there is something tangible to see.

"No, nothing like that. Although I am surprised that it hasn't happened yet. I just wanted to have an idea on where your knowledge about all that was. And..." I veer off, nervous about bringing up the topic. "I wanted to ask you about a mating bite. If you knew about that."

"Well, I've seen Flora's. But all I know is that it's a commitment thing, like getting married."

"Sort of," I sit down on a cushy armchair and pull her into my lap. "It's an acceptance, of sorts. When mates have found each other, and are happy to accept the bond, they seal it with a mating bite. It's an unbreakable commitment, a lot stronger than a marriage. It's a promise to one another also, to protect and care for one another."

"It sounds nice," she says, surprising me. "That level of commitment. Knowing that some one has irrevocably promised to have your back."

"If we were to... I mean, if I bit you like that, it would probably also trigger you to go into heat. Just so you are aware."

I start to run my fingers through the tangles in her hair to focus myself. "Sorry, I'm doing a horrible job of this. But I'm asking you if you would like my bite. I'm ready, I have been since I met you, but being with you all this time has only cemented that for me."

Chapter 38

R osie

I mull over his words.

Is that something I want? To be tied together like that?

If there is one thing that is certain, I am already tied to him. The moment we met my life changed course. There's no reason that I wouldn't want him in my life. Every day, he proves more and more that he is my perfect partner in every way.

"Yes."

"What? Really?" The hope in his eyes is a wondrous thing.

"Yes, Fin. I want your mating bite, to be tied to you forever."

He picks me up, jumping to stand and spinning me around with a peel of laughter, pure joy in his voice.

"I love you, Fin."

He pauses, holding me high and I wrap my legs around his waist, holding his face in my hands.

"I love you too."

Finnegan kisses me, and I pour all my love and feelings and emotions for him into it.

"I want it to be special." He says, setting me down on the ground.

"Look around you, *this* is pretty special." I laugh, pressing myself to him in a hug. "All I need is you."

Finnegan calls the lunch service, asking them to bring extra food in case I go into heat. He says that we will want to be left alone for up to a few days. I'm more grateful than ever that we are in this secluded villa.

He insists that I eat plenty of fruit and drink lots of water once the food arrives. It's cute that he's becoming even more doting all of a sudden.

"Will we get blood on the sheets?" I worry, when Finnegan guides me to the bed.

"No, sweetie. I will hardly take any of your blood. You don't need to worry about the bite part, you'll enjoy it I promise."

"I'm ready," I say, once I am cozy and sitting in his lap.

His eyes meet mine, intensity in his gaze as he speaks. "I love you, Rosie. I promise to protect you and care for you. You're mine."

"I'm yours," I whisper, barely a breath of volume to it as his words sink in.

Finnegan leans in, nuzzling my neck and breathing deeply. His tusks press into my neck as he opens his mouth wide, and I'm trapped, unable to move until he allows it again. His fangs prick my neck, but instead of pain, a pure and acute pleasure forms, shooting a straight line to my clit. My hips move of their own accord, grinding against him, pressing my pussy against his cock as he pulls away.

I drag him into a kiss, pure contentment filling me.

My mate.

Heat flushes along my body as I writhe against him, an arousal like no other flowing through me.

"I think it's happening." I pull back from our kiss to tell him.

I desperately try to pull my sundress over my head as the heat overwhelms me.

"Hey, stop. Breathe." Finnegan takes my dress from me, pulling it gently over my head. "It's OK, I've got you."

He lays me on the bed, moving between my legs and straight to my clit. My mate slides his tongue over me, burying his fingers in my pussy and works me through two separate orgasms.

But it's not enough, "I need you, Fin. I need you inside me."

He settles us back on the bed so I am straddling him, slipping his cock into my pussy and letting me writhe and grind against him. My hands are all over him, in his hair, around his neck, gripping his waist as I fuck him harder. He lets me wring my pleasure from him until it is too much and he is cumming inside me.

Crying from the intensity of all the orgasms, I still grind against him seeking release while he is pumping me full. Finally, a cool breeze whips in from the open door and the heat breaks.

My head starts to clear as I feel the warmth dissipating.

"There you are, that's it." My mate's soothing words float over my head as I collapse against him. "I have you, my love."

Epilogue

Rosie

Two months later.

Today is the day. The big grand opening of my new location.

The design team really knocked it out of the park with this one. The café is the perfect combination of my old decor and the new layout. We're even planning on stocking a grocer's section soon, with local produce from both the monster and human sides of the city so that we can make sure everyone has access to fun new things.

I look to my mate, getting the last few supplies set up, sorting paper coffee cups with my signature logo on them. He's wearing a dark wash pair of jeans and a t-shirt, his biceps on full display.

Finnegan has been growing out his hair, and he has it pulled back into a messy bun, a few strands falling loose. I never thought that I would be so attracted to his hair pulled back, but here we are.

"I got you something," I say, coming out of the utility room where we had our first kiss. I hold up the matching pink apron, made extra big to fit his giant form.

"Ha!" He grins, coming over and quickly snatching it from me. "I love it!"

I hop up on a step stool and put it over his head, careful not to further mess with his hair.

"Ro?" Flora's voice calls from out front.

"Flora!" I squeal, rushing to meet my friend. "I can't believe it's finally happening!"

Flora and Sebastian help us with the last few finishing touches. The rest of our friends joining once we officially open.

My three new hires all do the actual running of the café, me and Finnegan just chatting with the customers and our friends, helping out where needed.

Everyone is here, Flora's sound tech Hyacinth with her two mates. Liliana turned out to be a close colleague of Finnegan's and they've been hitting it off lately, now that they can relate over their Human mates. And Addison's work with Sebastian has made her and Flora close, therefore I've been hanging with her a lot now too.

Daisy and Cleo, who I've known for years, both give me a big hug when they see me. Their mates, a giant kraken who's even bigger than Finnegan and a minotaur, both hang out with us too. It's good to properly chat to Nereus and Maddox, I need to make more of an effort with them.

Even Aspis, the naga who I tried to flirt with at the party is here to support.

It's a full circle moment for my mate, seeing everyone together like this. I notice him tearing up at one point, looking around the room.

All of these people, this whole suburb of the city, it was all here because he took a chance. I couldn't be more proud of him.

The Zodiac Society

If you enjoyed this book, try out some of my other stories... Month one is free on my Patreon.

Twelve signs. Twelve creatures. One challenge that could change everything.

When a freshman astronomy student stumbles into a nightclub that doesn't exist on any map, she's not looking for magic. She's looking for somewhere—anywhere—to disappear. But what she finds instead is a shimmering pocket of enchantment hidden on campus: the Zodiac Society.

By morning, she's waking up in Zodiac House with a choice—forget what she saw and go back to her ordinary life, or take the Zodiac Challenge: seduce twelve paranormals aligned with the signs of the zodiac, and earn her place in the Society. The rules are outrageous. The reward? Power, freedom, and a new name: Astraea.

Her first assignment? Aries.

Blaze is a faun with smoldering eyes, a sadistic streak, and a taste for control. His element is fire—and he knows exactly how to wield it. In a night of sharp pain and blistering pleasure, Astraea is stripped down, opened up, and set ablaze—inside and out. She's never submitted to anyone before. She never knew she could.

But this challenge is more than a string of pleasure-filled encounters. As Astraea dives into this world of monsters, magic, and illicit seduction, she begins to feel a pull toward something deeper—especially from the three Society members tasked with guiding her through the challenge: cool, clever Winslow; golden-hearted Ellis; and commanding, mysterious Miles.

And beneath it all, her body is changing. Her senses are sharpening. Something inside her is waking up.

Astraea might have entered the Zodiac Society by accident. But she's not leaving by choice.

ARIES is a high-heat, monster romance novella set in a secret society of pleasure, magic, and transformation. Each novella in The Zodiac Society series features a new zodiac-inspired creature, a spicy standalone seduction arc, and a slow-burning emotional journey that culminates in a shared HEA.

You will receive a new short story, exclusive artwork, and a page straight from Astraea's secret journal every month!

A Note from Sofia

Thank you so much for deciding to pick up my book!

I write across the paranormal and omegaverse romance genres, please check out my other books if that interests you.

To stay in the loop, scan the QR code for my important links, or go to https://sofiaroseauthor.com/

To be updated of even more news, consider signing up to my newsletter on my website.

Zinnia

A bubbly café owner. A powerful orc alpha. One fated bond that starts with a single, stolen breath...

Rosie's not afraid of monsters. In fact, she's kind of into them—especially after seeing what love looks like for her best friend Flora. She's a little busy running her café and keeping the espresso machine from exploding... but if fate has a monster mate waiting for her, she's more than ready to meet him.

She just didn't expect to scent match with Finnegan—the sharply dressed, sweet-voiced orc alpha who handles label strategy for Fortune Records. And she definitely didn't expect it to happen at Flora's house, with flowers in her hand and zero time to process.

But Finnegan doesn't rush.

He's kind. Respectful. Filthy rich and devastatingly intense—but always patient. Instead of claiming Rosie, he takes her on dates. Sends her flowers. Earns her trust. And somewhere between sweet kisses and scorching heat, Rosie starts to fall for him... not because of a bond, but because he sees her.

Now all she has to do is let herself believe she deserves it.

If you love cozy monster romance, fated mates, cinnamon roll alphas, and spicy power-play with a soft center... you'll devour *Zinnia*.

F/M Monster x Human Romance

Fated Mates • Orc in a Suit • Millionaire Alpha

Primal Play • Pegging • Switch x Switch Kink

High Heat + Tender Wooing + Café Vibes

Zinnia is Book Four in the Fortune Records Omega-verse series - standalone HEAs, endless spice, and monstrous swoon every time.